£12

THE LAST OF UPTAKE

"Suddenly a flame blossomed out of it like a lovely flower, was joined by another, and yet more, till there was a bed of great petunias. They swayed in the moaning wind, these flowery flames; next there came a low rumble, sparks like fireworks for a victory, and the whole of Uptake was roaring and crackling."

THE
LAST OF UPTAKE

OR

THE ESTRANGED SISTERS

By

Simon Harcourt-Smith

Illustrated by

𝕽𝖊𝖝 𝖂𝖍𝖎𝖘𝖙𝖑𝖊𝖗

B. T. Batsford Ltd.
LONDON

For Rosamond

"*Vous qui possédez la beauté*
Sans être vaine ni coquette,
Et l'extrême vivacité
Sans être jamais indiscrète.
Vous à qui donnèrent les Dieux
Tant de lumières naturelles,
Un esprit juste, gracieux,
Solide dans le sérieux
Et charmant dans les bagatelles."

Voltaire

Made and printed in England at the Batsford Press

I

IT BLEW HARD FOR THREE DAYS; THEN THE WIND was smothered under a clinging sea-fog that caught it during the night. To Lady Tryphena's fancy the lighthouse guarding the Tentacles seemed to be singing the wind's dirge. Meanwhile the mist became tangled in the elms, twined under the pediment, set the stucco sweating. Drops of moisture as big as grapes fell and burst upon the flags in the colonnade; at times there fell with them bits of swallows' nests, or the plaster tip of some Emperor's nose. It all made a terrible mess; she must remember to speak to Hake about it; but the bits came down so fast, so suddenly, the flags were hardly swept before they were a disgrace again. Everything was suffering a humid dissolution. She had known days before that it would be so; her swollen joints had warned her.

Quite a large piece of plaster fell at her feet; at this rate of disintegration it was a mystery how Uptake had stood so long. Its slender columns, the statues, and all that shell-work were, you might have thought, too delicate to withstand even the weather of her lifetime, let alone the buffeting that they must have received in the previous hundred years, since the day when her wicked great-grandfather built the place. Yet she was bound to admit it was still a gentleman's, one might even say a nobleman's, mansion. Indeed it was supposed to be a show house, though, thank goodness, few of the curious came to gape at it these days. They went rather to look at Pinmoney, over the hill, especially since that old reprobate Fitzcollop had made the improvements, given it back its castle aspect. Of course, for the castle style much could be said, when it was a question of a family seat. Poor dear Deborah, Tryphena recalled, had only last week declared that it was more suitable than the foreign, one might say pagan, air of Uptake. True, Deborah with her indifferent health was a little apt to talk nonsense; yet perhaps on this occasion she was right. Tryphena shivered, then sighed. It was no use crying for the moon, thinking of improvements, when you were hard put to keep up decent fences.

5

Plummett came fussing up. "Well, I never did! Your Ladyship in this damp without a thing round her shoulders. As sure as I'm born, my Lady, you'll be catching your death one of these fine days." She went off, was back with a shawl in a trice. Like so many things in life, Tryphena remarked, the shawl came from India, from Kashmir; it had belonged to grandpapa, was still exquisitely soft and warm. But Plummett flung it on to her mistress's shoulders with gestures so violent, drew it so tight about the long thin throat, it seemed like a torture jacket. As she fiddled with it Plummett kept on murmuring, "Not so young as we was, not so young . . ." There hung, Tryphena noticed with distaste a drip to the end of Plummett's nose; on the hands, calloused by continual laundering, the veins were beginning to show up like seaweed; she puffed from the effort of standing on tiptoe to reach her mistress. Like poor dear Deborah, Tryphena remembered maliciously—and the detail restored her good humour—Plummett was a little short in the leg. But she hadn't one-tenth of even Deborah's stamina. You could not listen to that cough of hers all night without knowing it. As like as not, one day she would be just snuffed out in a wink of the eye; the lower orders were all the same —no powers of resistance; it was a question of breeding. Who was Plummett to talk of growing old?

"For pity's sake, Plummett, don't fidget!"

Plummett sprang back as if stung. For a moment the inflexible mouth was compressed into a martyred line. Habit, however, was too strong.

"Of course it is not for me to speak, but I'm sure Lady Deborah would have a return of her old trouble if she knew your Ladyship was out here in all kinds of weathers, exposed to these treacherous airs, and without a bonnet too. But I'm nothing but an old fidget, so your Ladyship will please excuse me."

She went off muttering; then Hake appeared, sneezing, his eyes running from the humid air. Trouble again, Tryphena supposed; no doubt before the week was out they'd have him on their hands with pneumonia. He had come to look very ancient and frail these last years; and he was growing, what one could only call, a little soft in the head; but the other day, hadn't they caught him, with a gigantic rusty pair of snuffers, trying to snuff the gas lamps in the Chinese saloon?

6

" . . . then Hake appeared . . . , his eyes running from the
humid air."

7

"Please, m'Lady." The poor thin whiskers curled downward under the weight of condensed moisture; the strange sing-song voice had grown very uncertain. He must be prodigious old, she thought. He had seemed ancient enough already when she and the others were children. "Hake's a monstrous funny fish," they would chant in chorus, mimicking the sing-song voice, "Hake's a monstrous funny fish," and then scuttle away down the cool vaulted corridors by the kitchen, past the laundry, the bakery, the stillroom that always smelt darkly of elderberry and dandelion wine, with Hake lumbering after, in his yellow wasp waistcoat, crying vengeance. She and Deborah wore muslin frocks with extravagant high waists, great blue sashes, and Leghorn straw hats that made them almost into grown-up misses; Matthew and Adolphus, poor dear things, had looked so handsome in their yellow nankeen suits, with tight trousers, and very diverting German hats, like stunted beavers, that were all the rage for boys at the time; they had strings that hung down behind with tassels to finish them off. She and Deborah used to pull the tassels pretending they were ringing for Florida water . . . and now the two boys were dead, Spain and Greece had killed them; there was nobody but poor Deborah and she and Hake left, and he going to pieces under her very eyes.

"Please, m'Lady, Titmarsh is here; he would like the favour of a word, at your Ladyship's convenience of course. He's waiting in the underhall." Hake paused, then coughed. "When you have finished with Titmarsh, m'Lady, perhaps you will visit Lady Deborah?"

"How is she this morning?"

"I did hear say that her night had been troubled. Those tubes again, I'm told, m'Lady. But there, it's not to be wondered at, at our time of life, if your Ladyship will pardon the observation. No, indeed." He shook his head dolefully as if the seed-cake for poor Deborah's funeral were already baking. "Not to be wondered at, not at all," he mumbled on; "we must all thank God on our bended knees if we get through this winter," he paused, "if we do"; his tone was almost voluptuous.

"At our time of life" indeed; she rarely had come upon such impudence as to lump her and Deborah with his grizzly generation. Age might be a telescope that foreshortened the years and brought

8

everything over sixty into one grey regiment; but this was too much.

"That will do, Hake, that will do." Hake began, she noticed with pleasure, to tremble under her gaze. "By-the-by, Hake, I've been very put out lately at the way the plate is being neglected; the other day when the Bishop and Lord and Lady Conchwater were to dinner I was mortified, yes, mortified, by the state of the Trafalgar épergne."

That, she reflected with relish, as she watched Hake drag himself off, that should keep him in his place for a long time.

II

TO REACH THE UNDERHALL YOU TOOK ONE OF the outside flights of steps which, as they descended from the colonnade, curved back on themselves like the ends of a true-lover's knot. You went in again by a door with diamond panels of glass which were a mortuary for flies; a few abandoned bluebottles paraded like sextons among the corpses.

The underhall was also known, when visitors came, as the Museum. It was a welter of bric-à-brac, busts and show-cases and Indian presents amassed by her grandfather. There were late Roman statues (some of them seemed scandalously pagan), collected by her great-grandfather, the wicked Lord Winterbourne, and to house which he had constructed Uptake; a number of battered fragments in Rudimentary Style that poor Adolphus had discovered in Greece on his last fatal journey; cabinets of coins, cameos, Etruscan vases (poor Adolphus was responsible for most of these too). But the place was largely given over to the trophies and presents that grandpapa had brought home from India. Scattered about the room was a set of ivory chairs, carved, under Italian guidance, in a shape current in Europe at that date, but inlaid in black with views of a tiger-hunt, or the more embarrassing details of some heathen ritual. The cases were filled with outlandish decorations, sapphires poised like humming-birds on branches of the slenderest enamel, jade spoons the colour of the mist outside, with rubies burning in the tips of their handles, jewelled swords, and elephant howdahs of gold, jewel-encrusted.

9

" . . . a nobleman's mansion."

Amid these outlandish gee-gaws stood Titmarsh the gardener, his feet firmly planted in his top-boots; one hand, shaped and coloured like a bacon-flitch, held a hat that must have come from his grandfather, for it still bore traces of a three-cornered shape. There could have hardly existed a setting less appropriate to him than this. Yet Tryphena in her stiffening heart understood why he always held to being seen there. It would have been infinitely more convenient to talk to him on the terrace, or in the estate room. Nevertheless, she could not remember a time when she had spoken of the garden with Titmarsh elsewhere but here, or in the Indian hot-house, that crescent of glass which had been the toy of the first Marquess; ending in pavilions that were nothing but glades of stone palm trees, it was reserved for the Indian and tropic plants that were Titmarsh's pride.

These, the Museum, and the little lodge where he lived, a building in the Indian manner again with a domed roof carried on stone palm trunks and with bells hanging from the eaves: these were the only points at which he would come indoors. He preferred his garden and the park to any habitation; but an exception was made for the underhall, the Indian hot-house, and his lodge, for, said Titmarsh, they put you in mind of foreign parts.

Foreign parts, exotic fancies obsessed him. He was in this, Tryphena recalled, the very antithesis of his father, who going from Uptake as a young man to make an English, or as they called it Anglo-Chinese, garden for the Duc de Praslin, did not cease to regret his native groves, the wild uplands; he came home at last, finding nothing good in France save the Duke's watch, a marvel, he said, in a crystal case no thicker than a florin; it went for a year and told the day of the month, the phases of the moon, the tides; it also played two waltzes, a gavotte, and a march called "Frivolités Militaires".

Yes, the son was a very different kettle of fish. To roam the world, to flirt with the extraordinary had been from the first his passion. Tryphena remembered how when her parents had taken her abroad once as a school girl, and Titmarsh, then a gardener's boy, had been granted a holiday, they had found him one afternoon outside Rome lying exhausted on the Appian Way, in the shade of a cypress tree. On foot he had followed the Roman road that ran along the ridge above Uptake, going as far as Colchester, then

11

through France and down to Rome, by Roman roads all the way, as if he were a returning legionary. They had given him some money, and he had strode off to see Tivoli, and back by way of Florence and the Boboli Gardens and Genoa, with the fantastic conceits of Pegli. Ever after he had lost interest in good plain English gardening. This morning, for example, when Tryphena banished his smile with her just complaints of empty urns upon the terraces, down the alleys, his wrinkled brown face turned sulky.

"I dare say, my Lady, as we could scrape together a few geraniums for them urns; but geraniums never looks truly elegant; you won't be pleased, my Lady, with them, not if I lives my full span of years, you won't. Now, if we could pot out in winter the sort of flowers they has at Bobbly," he sighed at the thought of Italy, "then it 'ud be a different pair of shoes like. But bein' as Uptake's Uptake, and Bobbly's Bobbly, geraniums it must be, and no satisfaction for nobody."

He slapped his three-cornered hat dolefully against his leather breeches, as if to indicate that in England flower-gardening was a shameful waste of time. And so in his heart of hearts he believed, Tryphena knew. For him in northern climes his art must be confined to landscape gardening, the care of prospects and follies, or a humid treasury under glass. No sweet williams, nor red-hot pokers, nor love-in-the-mist for him. He snorted at the modern tenderness for what he called "cottage weeds", leaving the bedding-out round the house to Tim and his assistants; and a pretty mess they made of it. But the hot-house—ah! that was a different affair entirely, there was something for a good gardener's craft. In that still remote world where the living green leaves hung as quiet as the dead stone ones, and there was no movement save in a hissing pipe, or in moisture that dropped like a fat frog into the waterbutt: there Titmarsh moved with the inconsequent precision of a dream, stroking some monstrous velvet calix, or a leaf pale and fleshy as a negro's lip. He lived for his tropic blooms that evoked the spices and music of islands he would never see. They were most of them growing a trifle tired these days, his blooms, for they were descended from the cuttings brought home in triumph by the first Marquess long, so very long ago. Yet looking at them, Tryphena, who had never been in India, felt she had

12

caught her grandfather's rapture at the first sight of such curiosities. . . .

Titmarsh brought from behind his back the great hand that was free of any hat. He held in it a spray of enormous white unwinking blooms, that seemed to stare with the awful gravity of children.

"Looks you squarely in the eye, don't they, my Lady," his voice quavered with pride as he offered them, "the finest I've ever grown, though I says it. Now if your Ladyship takes good care of them, looks after 'em well, as the saying is, there bain't no telling how long they'll last." He shuffled his feet.

"But the hot-house—ah! that was a different affair entirely."

13

"Well, Titmarsh, what is it?"

"Begging your Ladyship's pardon, don't let them maids get at them, or there'll be no telling!"

The strange flowers seemed to take in everything, the showcases, the dusty marbles, the piers that bore the thrust of the columns from the vast hall above. The petals glowed in the half-dark with an almost blue light. Had they first appeared so to grandpapa Indus, that memorable night nearly a century ago, when, through some jungle by the great river from which he later took his title, he had led a desperate little band of scallywags to victory over the Nizam of Rak, and his fantastic host? Or had he merely come upon them as he flirted in the gardens of Government House at Calcutta with some lovely creature—not the admirable if slightly vulgar Miss Bouncer, the best catch in the whole of India: her father had shaken the pagoda tree with a vengeance and no mistake—whom he had married, and upon whose lakhs the family had lived ever since—till the disaster of poor Adolphus's wake, that was to say? And who was she, Tryphena, to pass judgment on the blame for that?

Titmarsh waited quietly as she mused. He was used to these long bursts of silence from her Ladyship, especially this last year or so. The forehead, so surprisingly smooth when at peace, was now ploughed with stern furrows, the high nose trembled fiercely. But the fierceness was self-directed. Who was she, puffed up with false pride, she thought with disgust, to call her grandmother vulgar, when she had never seen her? A merchant's daughter, true enough, who had thought herself lucky to marry the conqueror of Rak and become a marchioness; but without Miss Bouncer the Caudles would not still be at Uptake. After all, wicked great-grandfather Winterbourne had beggared the estate with his extravagant follies; and when grandpapa had gone off to India to try his fortune he'd possessed little save a derelict Uptake and a name that merely served to make life for him more expensive than it need have been. It wasn't, moreover, as if he had particularly distinguished himself at first. He had, it seemed, possessed a bit of his father's extravagant humours, which were hardly to the liking of a pompous Council; in his first campaign he had soon been given the humble duty of marching back to prison a pack of the most miserable ruffians, deserters, insubordinate rogues that

14

". . . a model of sisterly affection."

could be imagined. On the banks of the Indus this company had of a sudden stumbled upon the Nizam, with a force that out-numbered them thirty to one. Some of the rogues had been for flight, but grandpapa had argued till it was too late and all retreat cut off. He had then led his crew by night through a strange jungle —how he did it, Tryphena reflected, was a mystery, since in after life he could, according to common repute, be relied upon to lose his way if he walked between his house in Whitehall and Brooks's; but on this occasion it was an undisputed fact that he had led his tattered band by night, and without a blunder, round the Nizam's left flank, stole into the elephant lines, tied sprigs of burning hay to the ridiculous tails, and stampeded the beasts screaming with fright through the drowsy host.

The stratagem, born of a desperate fancy, proved a success that almost appalled its author by its magnitude. He had thought no further than a diversion to cover a discreet retirement; instead, grandpapa Winterbourne had found himself at dawn the master of the field, with his bullies metamorphosed into heroes, speeding their villainous carcases in full cry after a broken foe. The French artillery experts, the clockwork-tiger that mauled a clockwork Englishman, had availed the Nizam little; as he fell back his belly was split open by the dagger of a vengeful sweeper; the proud but luckless captain expired with dignity, striving to rally the abject hordes who were cut down in their retreat by his hurrying servants and necromancers. When night fell on the second day's pursuit, grandpapa, swaying a trifle in the saddle from fatigue and from answering the multitude of toasts that had been drunk to him, found himself the master of a dominion two-thirds the size of France. He was for a time bewildered by this incredible turn of fortune; but he soon discovered his wits, soon enough discreetly to resist most of the fabulous temptations that were put in his way by the frightened inhabitants. It was about the time of the un-pleasantness in Oudh, and the servants of the Company, even when conquering heroes, were ringed about with danger of enquiries from a suspicious House of Commons. Grandpapa Winterbourne had consequently behaved with the utmost prudence in Rak, and had provided for the future by marrying the heiress, Miss Bouncer. This restraint had won him almost universal honour. The mar-quisate had been its tangible reward, that and a statue of him in

16

toga and laurel-wreath, as Scipio Africanus, that was put up by his admirers in the square before the Nizam's silver Italian palace at Iskanderpatam; the statue, reputed to be a spirited work, had perished in the famous earthquake thirty years later, but grandpapa Winterbourne (or rather Indus now) was by then past caring about such things. He had lost all sense of reality where India came into question. For him reality was his querulous liver now, the tantrums of his lovely Creole mistress, Madame Letellier, the vapours of his Marchioness, the languors and absurd fancies of his daughters, that had almost carried off both of them into a decline. India was the escape from these vexations, a land half dreamed, half remembered, which he kept to himself, described only in the safety of his granddaughters' nursery.

"I'd have you imagine," he would command, settling Tryphena upon his thin knee, "I'd have you imagine, my lady, a country where there are no impudent linkmen, nor rumbling hackney coaches, but instead, when a person of quality has reason to journey, he floats with the greatest comfort and elegance in a painted barge, beneath a rich canopy, upon a majestic stream four times as mighty as the Thames at Greenwich. Ingenious musicians attend him with the sweetest airs that can be devised, curious birds with wings of emerald and ruby delight the trees, while ladies wear jewellery made out of minute and ravishing feathers, or glittering stars that turn by means of small machines concealed inside 'em. At night the flowers shine through the dark with the radiance and scent of a loved form half forgotten." He would cut short, and carry her off to the hot-house, to gaze, so far as she could recall, upon just such blooms as Titmarsh now offered her. Secretly she had liked them little; she had found them frightening and large; a bunch of cowslips was at that time almost too big for her hands. "When you're a grown lady of beauty and fashion," her grandpapa had gone on, "some sighing adorer will see such flowers as these gleaming through the dark, and they'll fill his mind with your image; but you, of course, young puss"—here he would pinch her cheek lightly—"you, of course, will have forgotten the youth long since, and be off elsewhere, with a train of shattered hearts behind you, and lying before, marriage to the handsomest, fittest suitor in the kingdom."

Instead, she thought ruefully, she had turned out a withered old spinster; few hearts had ever beat wildly for her; nor had hers for anyone—save once, and she had long since disciplined herself never, but never to think on that folly. . . .

III

TITMARSH AT LENGTH GREW RESTLESS, BEGAN to eye the misty park outside. "The wind," he coughed to rouse his mistress, "the wind's been and made a proper mess in the Wilderness, my Lady. There be a mighty branch of elm, a fair monster, down on the ruined bridge an' smashed a great bit out of un." He paused. "What's more, my Lady, the Wood-cutter 'us been upset. I'd be gratified if your Ladyship would give herself the trouble of having a look at him."

"There were sphinxes everywhere . . ."

18

Titmarsh was already making for the door, opening it for her. As Tryphena passed through she stared severely at him, stopped. "No, Titmarsh, I am vastly occupied this morning. Such trifles can well wait on a more suitable time."

"There now, my Lady, that were just what I were a-thinking, as the saying is. I says to myself, Titmarsh, I says, her Ladyship 'ull never have any time this morning to gallivant about the park, however much the old wind may have harmed it. Besides, I says, if your Ladyship will pardon the liberty, it be far too raw a morning for her Ladyship to take chances like. We don't want her to be laid up same as poor dear Lady Deborah."

Though she saw well enough through its crudity, Titmarsh's cunning defeated her. She called for her pélisse. It was delightfully warm, of fur, *à la Polonaise*, cut on the model of a hussar's cape. Years ago, when she had first had it, Vanity still nibbled at her, she had fancied herself vastly in it. She had seen herself, the pélisse flung elegantly about epaulettes, she on a white charger, like the late Empress of Russia, leading her Household Troops desperately through a snowy capital. Now she only wondered whether the pélisse would suffice to keep away from her old bones the chill of a misty park.

When she was ready to go out "I'd have you know, Titmarsh," she said, "that I'm not, I'm certainly not coming to see the damage that the park has suffered. I want to visit with you the places where the new daffodil bulbs must be planted. I'm extremely vexed with that lazy Tim for not having put them in before. I doubt but that it's not too late in the season now. Nevertheless," and she fixed Titmarsh with a stern eye, "I must be just. It's not really Tim's fault, idle though he may be; for he never gets any guidance from you; and as he has no head of his own . . . ."

"That's just what I were a-going to say, my Lady. No head at all has that silly lad. I were putting him to work on the Dancers yesterday as the saying is, and before my back was turned he had 'em dancing backwards. It fair makes you weep. . . . Not but what I haven't put them to rights, so that they be working like a marvel for all to see, as I hopes your Ladyship will agree when I shows 'em shortly. But it weren't half a job, that it weren't."

Instead of the sky, or regiments of oaks to guide them, there was only the shifty mist, sidling everlastingly round them till Tryphena

19

became confused and leaned heavily upon her stick. It was one that her grandpapa had given her, at an age so light-footed and sure it had seemed impossible she would have any need for a prop. It was not the best of grandpapa Indus's canes. It didn't, for instance, play a tune, nor tell the time, nor carry a compass and snuff-box in its handle. But it was stout enough and most suitable to an elderly person of quality. The calamander-wood shaft, for all its black-and-white elegance, had the toughness of the Indian jungle about it; it was one more link (though such a thought was not admitted to her privacy), one more link binding her to the glowing forests that she, like Titmarsh, would never see. The handle was a gold and jewelled sphinx. It fitted neatly into her stiff, painful grasp.

Sphinxes. There were sphinxes everywhere, a small gold one in her hand, great stone beasts lining the drive and the terraces,

"It's all an unhappy mistake . . ."

20

staring out into the mist and perhaps seeing more there than she did. How annoyed poor dear Adolphus used to grow with their anatomy when he came back from his travels!

"It's all an unhappy mistake," he would cry, very excited (her dead brother's image was almost painful in its clarity—the ringing voice, the shake of the head to free the noble forehead of some ingratiating curl), "all a mistake. For once we must concede that the Greeks were wrong. The Sphinx was a man, not a female. But it was the Egyptians who first fell into confusion. Let me tell you how; I can promise you a story of the highest interest...." He would launch off into an explanation so intricate, nobody would attempt to understand him; instead the band of them, his enfeebled mother, two doting sisters, his elder brother, would sit in ecstasy at his feet, transported by admiration, not listening to a word, till they would suddenly hear his proposal that the old sphinxes they knew, the sphinxes upon whose round bosoms three generations of Caudles had sharpened their penknives, should be refashioned to give them a masculine air, or thrown away, and replaced by correct ones which Adolphus would model from Assyrian precedents. A squabble would start, voices would rise, and peace only be brought back by the intervention of her father.

He would pass suddenly, an ill-defined gentle figure always dressed in black, with a red box, full, no doubt, of government secrets, tucked neatly under his arm. His ministerial cares, his preoccupation with bringing the government in or out would vanish for a time; he would intervene softly in the quarrel, the sphinxes which wicked great-grandfather had sown about the park never changed their sex; yet Adolphus would be left with the impression that his father really agreed with him. . . .

They had reached the bridge now that spanned the ravine between the house and the Wilderness. It was an affair of the greatest audacity and elegance that took in one strong leap the respectable distance between the two banks. From the river below the bridge seemed to be flying in the sky. Adolphus always used to say that it reminded him of paintings by a Frenchman called Robert. What queer names French painters habitually had, Tryphena thought, when she was young. Robert, David, Gerard: Christian names, that was what it amounted to, as if they were so many footmen. Nowadays in France the fashion for calling yourself

21

so fancifully seemed to have died out. Perhaps, even, there were no painters any more. It might well be so, with the general dissolution that was now going on. . . .

On the summit of the bridge she stopped. At first it was very still, so that there seemed nothing left in the world save the glistening balustrade, Titmarsh's impatient hat, turned grey now under a thousand beads of wet, the wet mist that encircled and clutched at her throat like a fatal scarf. Titmarsh's boots, as they stamped the cold into the bridge, made the only sound in a moist Creation. Then, as she waited, her isolation began to retreat; a puff of air, bearing, for all its misty burden, a scent of remotely burning wood, and nearer seaweed, unveiled, for an instant, like some sly showman in a fair, the naked outline of an elm on the opposite bank. There were suddenly a thousand neglected sounds, a colt whinnying from fright against the mist in one of the paddocks, a far-off clatter of saucepans, and from deep down below the urgent gibberish of the river, swollen by water as brown as the saucepans, water that clamoured and blustered, with all the absurd impatience of rich travellers, to be sped on its way. Angrily it was storming the quiet pools, where on summer afternoons the trout hung as motionless as the clouds; it was ranting about the boulders, this short-tempered rainwater, when a little patience would send it slipping round their smoothed flanks as easily as dolphins dive through white horses. And after it had come to the slow black estuary, what then? Nothing but a deserved climax to futility; a miserable seeping into the sea with all powers dispersed through a host of noxious serpentine channels; the litter of the valley, last year's nest, the lock of loved hair now grown odious, the murderer's handkerchief, crawling through the ranks of one-legged sea-birds that waited for the tide to change.

Titmarsh blew through his hands. "Your Ladyship were always a rare one for lingering on this bridge; particularly when there were a bit of mist hanging about." He spoke almost reproachfully, as if this lingering were a vile habit like nailbiting or backbiting, which throughout a lifetime he had vainly tried to cure. "But who had the way of doing it worse than your Ladyship were poor Lord Adolphus, God rest his soul." Titmarsh touched his hat, but whether to God or to Adolphus's shade Tryphena did not know.

It was true enough. Rarely would the mist close down in those

22

"An affair of the greatest audacity and elegance."

23

days that were now more remote than China but that Adolphus and she would scurry out of the schoolroom, leaving poor Miss Hemlock calling to her echo the roll of English Kings, or pleading with the thickening air to give correctly the date of the sea-fight at Aegospotami. By roundabout sweating paths they would reach the bridge; arrogant in their redoubt of mist, they would listen to the cries for them go lurching wide like ill-aimed, spent cannon-balls. Then the bridge would become the prow of the Argosy, the mist would be the secret Pontus, Adolphus, draped in an old blanket they kept hidden in a nearby pavilion, would be Jason, elegant and fearless under his romantic white cloak; while she was proud to act the faithful crew. For a time they would peer into the obscurity ahead, that held the Gods alone knew what supernatural dangers; then from the estuary would come such a rasping endless lament as the feeble air now bore her: a noise as of a prisoner's poor file vainly grinding against his bars: it was the complaint of hungry gulls at low tide.

The sound would draw Adolphus to his full height (he was exceptionally tall for his age); it would set the nostrils quivering in that noble nose which, though shaped like hers, was yet small enough to embellish his charming face.

"Hark!" he would cry, and the word would submerge her in a wave of delicious dread. "Hark! I hear land ahead. Back water, my brave bullies, back water, and then rest on your oars while I swim ashore and spy out the coast."

She would plead almost with tears for leave to go too. How could he leave his silly ship without crew? he would ask superbly. Besides, he wanted no cry-babies with him. In a flash he would be over the balustrade, tearing his fine frilled shirt as he hung there, filling Tryphena with a mixed terror born of the unknown horrors that the Pontus held and the known height of the bridge above the stream. She would shriek, and bring the searching grown-ups upon them. There would be nothing but gruel for supper and Adolphus not speaking to her; while Deborah, neat and tidy among the pleasures of her mother's medicine bottles, would titter in a superior, odious manner.

To Titmarsh's evident relief, she finally walked on. As she reached the end of the bridge she peered down into the furred mystery of the ravine. It was certainly a curiosity, this great

24

unreasonable cleft in the smooth earth, with the slender stream winding through the middle of it. She shared with poor dear Deborah a taste for reading of far countries; and the likeness, on a reduced scale of course, to the Grande Cañon was obvious to both of them. The idea had blossomed a few summers ago, one blistering July day when the withered grass had exposed a purple earth, and the watercourse below had trembled in the haze like the toes of ballet dancers. But after the horrified recognition of their common conceit the sisters had never again referred to it. For it evoked with a sharpness altogether unbearable the whole tragedy of poor unwise, one might almost say poor criminal, Henry.

A few years since she would have used the word criminal without hesitation; still now, despite anything that those unpleasant solicitors might say, there was no denying his intentions had bordered upon the criminal, even if his actions could be more charitably construed. Yet, it was a sad enough thing to contemplate, the actual Marquess of Indus afraid to return to his own country, and in consequence living a miserable mountebank's existence in a rough continent; far from taking there the position that his ancestors had won for him, he was driven to hawking his nobility before the curious riff-raff in the outlandish mining camps, the tinsel cities of Mexico and Western America.

"Don't goggle at me, Titmarsh," she cried testily, determined to put an end to her thoughts. Titmarsh swallowed apologetically; his eyes had not been upon his mistress; they had instead been absorbed by the image of a royal garden in Spain that he had recently heard of, where a group of stone horses, submerged in a pool except for their nostrils, emitted through that dry extremity a plume of water rising one hundred and fifty feet into the mountain air, and which could be admired from a distance of seven miles. Now such a device as that was what a garden urgently needed; and yet her Ladyship bothered about geraniums. But nothing elegant or important could be done about the place without a man to give the orders. It was a thousand pities that his Lordship did not come back and live, as he should do, at Uptake. It was altogether a queer business. Of course, his Lordship had liked his little joke, and he could not, perhaps, carry his liquor like his forefathers. But there was no harm in him and he ought to come back, however nice and well-spoken the ladies might be.

25

If the bridge was Adolphus's, at the end of it you entered wicked great-grandpapa's world, order tempered by a carelessness so elaborate, it became the height of art. The winding alleys, the broken columns, the sudden glades and plumed fountains all followed a design as precise as it was subtle. Here in some misty clearing you came perhaps upon a little pavilion, that with its tric-tracs, umbrellaed sages, its dragons menacing among bells,

"a little pavilion . . . best suited to adorn the shores of a Soochow lake."

seemed best suited to adorn the shores of a Soochow lake; round a bend of the path a replica of some well-known ruins in the Forum loomed up, to ram home all the old platitudes about vanity, and the ultimate dissolution; the moss that grew over the carefully crumbled stonework had, Tryphena recalled, been imported at some cost from the Engadine. . . .

The alleys were bathed in wet vapour; despite the shelter of their yew alcoves, the stone nymphs were bearded with dew, like horrid women in fairs; only one of them had escaped the beard; perhaps it was because she represented winter and half hid her shining limbs beneath a stony coat. Tryphena almost chuckled; it was an edifying enough thought.

Titmarsh, walking ahead, a vague blot upon the chaste white of the mist, suddenly called:

"Now, my Lady, if you please, look you here. Tidy mess them trees've made, and no mistake."

No. Titmarsh had not exaggerated. The wind had indeed made a horrible mess. In some places there were whole trees down; but most of the damage had been worked by the fall of huge limbs off those treacherous elms that she had wanted to fell years ago. It was Deborah's sentimentality that had saved them, and now Tryphena wished that Deborah would come to see the result. A great branch had, true enough, crashed across the ruined bridge and worked havoc with it. The picturesque air was quite gone, leaving it merely dilapidated. How cast down wicked great-grandpapa would have been by the sight; he had lavished a particular love upon his ruined bridge; two paintings and no less than five engravings of it adorned the walls of Uptake; and now it was ruined in earnest, or so it would seem. . . .

The ice-house, pyramidal and moss-grown, loomed mysterious before her. When Tryphena was small there had been for her a regular ceremony each winter of accompanying the ice-blocks as they were cut out of the lake, down the alleys that dripped in a humid chorus just as they did now, down into the glacial secrets of the pyramid. She would forget the muddy paths, the northern vapours, and fancy herself involved in some awful Egyptian rite. She would sing a snatch of a rather difficult song her governess had lately put her to work upon, and which seemed peculiarly appropriate to the occasion: "O Isis and Osiris" it began, but how it went on now escaped her, though, she recalled, it had greatly impressed her at the time. The queer conceits of childhood! The ice-house was never used now; the lake was clogged up with weeds, and nobody lived any longer at Uptake whose blood found the weather ever hot enough for ice. But when you were fifteen, and the winter seemed endless, you needed only to steal the rusty key of the ice-house, open the mysterious triangular door, suddenly inhale the scent of sacking and dry cold that came from within, and the wet humours of winter were dispelled, across the meadows the scythes whistled in great blue arcs, the thick woods hummed like cities, there would be summer pudding or iced raspberry fool for dinner. . . . Perhaps one day, when poor Henry was mercifully dead and young Lucius had succeeded, bringing back with him to Uptake some of Adolphus's joy (for he had inherited much of his dear father's gaiety), then perhaps there would once again live at Uptake people with bones that were sometimes released from winter's grasp, gentlemen who would mop their brows in all the vigour of their age and call for their wine to be chilled on July evenings; and young girls in crisp muslins who would lower their long eyelashes over glasses of iced sherbert, to mask the effect of gallant vows, though their heaving bosoms would yet betray them to the practised eye.

"One danged great branch," called Titmarsh with melancholy out of the gloom ahead, "'us been and knocked the ball off'n the ice-house top. It'll be a proper job to mend it nice-like, but I reckon your Ladyship'll want it put all ship-shape again, though there bain't any call for ice these days?"

"Yes, Titmarsh, of course. Of course. I'm truly surprised by such a question. You know it's our duty, our trust to keep everything in perfect order for those who come after. That we must do with all the poor means we possess."

"Just what I be always a-saying, my Lady, and there never were a truer word spoken. Wherefor I've been at them pains to mend the Dancers so proper; and your Ladyship 'ud want me to do no less by the Wood-cutter, more so being as he bain't in such a sorry way as them were, no, not by a long cry."

The alley turned here, she remembered, and then the aviary was in front of you. Yes, there it rose, as fragile, fantastic as some figment of an opium-dream. The delicate trelliswork glistened

28

" . . . the glacial secrets of the pyramid."

29

with a moisture that hid the ravages of rust, though the bells under the pagoda eaves might have been silenced by it. This airy construction had been devised to house great-grandpapa's curious birds, brilliant macaws from the Jesuits' Musical Kingdom on the banks of the Paraguay, impudent parrakeets from the Spice Islands, crested hoopoes from China, and from the remote state of Ava gaudy pheasants that were already half turkeys. Wicked great-grandpapa had spent a fortune upon them. For such curiosities he had been the best client of India House in his day; indeed, this passion of his had established for him the friendly relations with the Company that later secured for grandpapa the way to Indian wealth. In fact—and Lady Tryphena smiled among the cold, weeping branches—this rusty old aviary might be considered to be the foundation of the Indus fortunes.

"Best tread prudent-like, my Lady, it be powerful muddy just here."

Titmarsh's voice came as if from the other side of the world. Though he could hardly see her, he sensed that she might easily slip, lost as he knew her to be once again in her musings. And indeed she was still thinking of the rusty aviary and how she could remember it when it had yet been as bright as the plumage of its prisoners, whose ranks grandfather Indus had constantly reinforced. Her father, angel though he was, had never been able to see all the way from Westminster, over his barricade of red boxes and State papers, as far as a rusting aviary that every Spring housed a slenderer company of aged and cynical fowl. Then there had been all those deaths, her father's and darling Adolphus's (of which after all these years she still could not trust herself to think without tears), and of course poor brother Matthew being killed so suddenly, and his lovely Caroline following him so quickly to the grave, and the title with an impoverished Uptake passing to unfortunate baby Henry; and nothing but trouble in the upbringing of him; two weak old maids striving to curb his coarse and wicked tastes. No wonder the old aviary, like so much else of Uptake's former glories, had been woefully neglected. But perhaps when charming young Lucius succeeded he would revive its splendours, cause the forlorn garden once again to flash with the gleam of tropic wings, and songs that could be hardly less bright. . . .

"Here he lies," Titmarsh suddenly cried; "it weren't no branch

30

this time as done it. He were just plain lifted off his pedestal by the wind's strength and nothing else."

The Wood-cutter lay forlorn in the crushed grass, the once gaudy colours of his wooden clothes turned grey by the wet. When all was right with him he stood upon a rusty socket, a look of staring amiability upon his handsome face, in his hands a sharp axe; you pulled a string, the axe would be flashed high over his broad-brimmed hat and would descend with the nicest precision and force to split any log of reasonable size that you might care to place in position. Once, Tryphena remembered, Adolphus and she had built a rabbit hutch out of wood originally chopped by the Wood-cutter.

The figure was yet another of wicked great-grandpapa's conceits. In his time he had peopled the gardens with automata; he had been possessed by a veritable passion for them. Many had dis-

"a look of staring amiability upon his handsome face."

31

appeared; there had been a number that Tryphena's mother had tactfully described as unsuitable; these had been removed, and were kept in a padlocked storeroom into which nobody in Tryphena's time had dared to penetrate (she had often caught herself wondering about their exact nature and, ashamed, had turned her mind elsewhere . . .). Then others had been broken beyond repair until there now remained only the Dancers, the Wood-cutter, lying at present in distress at her feet, and the Sage whose mechanism was, of course, disconnected.

"He's still got a bit of life in him," Titmarsh muttered; pulling a brass key from his pocket, he put it into a hole between the Wood-cutter's shoulder-blades and began to wind. Then he tugged the string, almost brutally it seemed to Tryphena; there was a rattle and then a buzz; the Wood-cutter began to twitch and strain convulsively, raising the axe and straightening his back in futile effort. His struggles there on the wet ground put you for all the world in mind of a tall pheasant expiring at the feet of the gun that had brought him crashing down. Men, when they were shot, doubtless looked no less grotesque than the poor Wood-cutter, and they, luckless things, so rarely had an ingenious Titmarsh to mend them.

"Don't you worry too hard for him, my Lady; we'll set him to rights. First thing to-morrow we'll take that silly young Tim off the beds to lend me a hand."

Once again the proper upkeep of the garden would be neglected; Tryphena did not, however, protest, for she knew it to be useless. Titmarsh was the one person at Uptake who, she was well aware, did not fear her.

"And now, my Lady, if you please, we'll just have a look at the Dancers."

It was almost a command. Titmarsh seemed to realise this, for he quickly added, "I reckon your Ladyship'll be that gratified."

IV

THEY WALKED DOWN A FLAGGED PATH THAT made the tap of her stick bound crazily through the mist, or so it seemed to her. They passed the Maze, dank and fearful now with the four Italian comedians in stone to mock you at the entrance, Pulcinello, Sganarelle, the Doctor, and the Spanish Captain. Dimly she glimpsed the Chinese Roundabout; it was out of order, the machinery had jammed; since it did not obsess him as did the automata, Titmarsh could not be brought to repair it, though its ills were doubtless of the simplest sort. The golden hoopoe was missing from the summit of the roof, the phœnix-and-dragon cars hung awry as if grounded on the shoals of mist.

"Careful, my Lady, careful. There be a monstrous big trunk down across the path here. Missed the grotto by a hand's-breadth. Fair chawed up the ground, so it did."

The wicked bark of the monster gleamed as dark as the depths of the ocean from which it might well have come. Titmarsh gave a hand at once rough and respectful to help her over it. As she adjusted the pélisse she suddenly saw by how little the grotto had escaped. One great tentacle of a branch had in its fall glanced along a flying buttress, crumbling the strange pumice-like stone of which it was built, bringing down a shower of the petrified sea-shells that adorned it. The once elegant gate in the arch of the buttress, commanding the entrance to the grotto, had been wrenched by the shock off its frail hinges and leant outwards, an eternal spectator of the mist.

"We'll just take a look inside, Titmarsh. The grotto has many happy memories for me."

That was quite untrue. It had always terrified her childhood, ever since her grandfather first told her of Pluto's dark kingdom and how Persephone was carried down into it. There was nothing dark about the grotto; its pearly walls glowed with a secret light, as if all the million sea-shells that went to make them still held something of their phosphorescent seas—but for all that, Tryphena

33

as a child had lived in constant terror of meeting Pluto and his grisly court advancing round one of the curved passages.

When she grew up, the place had seemed to her merely absurd; she had never understood in those days why the Prince, when he brought the Russian Emperor to Uptake, should have insisted upon the banquet being given in the grotto. It had provoked endless trouble with the servants, let alone her mother's famous relapse. Vexed by the whole affair, Tryphena had shunned the grotto ever since, but now she was suddenly filled with a whim to revisit its fantastic chambers, to look again with shocked eyes upon the bath where that shameless Italian dancer La Fiorina, a hundred years before, had, in front of a chosen company it is true, exposed herself to a public admiration no less warm than the water in which she reclined.

The fungoid furniture in the first saloon and the pendent stalactites of disquieting shape had never failed in the past to put Tryphena out; to-day they recalled something she had seen at the play when she had been very small, at Drury Lane or Astley's perhaps. Half the fantastic windows were shattered, some of the artificial cobwebs were reduced to miserable threads, while grey real ones flourished in the least appropriate corners; there was a smell of fox, and from several of the stalactites the shells and spar had fallen away so they looked for all the world like witches undressed. Yet for the first time this dilapidated room enwrapped her in an enchantment so poignant she could hardly breathe, and feared a renewal of her asthma. She was not aware of the sphinx's head cutting into her thin hand from the force with which she lent upon the stick. She could only smell the reek of oil lamps that set the grown-ups sweating in their furs. As the prince bent to kiss his predestined love, the gauze curtains rose one by one, the castle came awake, and the orchestra was like a soothing storm. Then there was sleet in the theatre doorway and the surly linkman would not find their carriage; Miss Hemlock would fuss at her for looking untidy and Adolphus jeer because she had cried for the princess's cruel lot. Why, why had she not died before the last gauze curtain lifted? Or perhaps it had been merely a cobweb, and she as silly in youth as she now was in age.

The grotto was contrived in the shape of a snail's shell, with passages that spiralled inward from room to room. There was a

"The alleys were bathed in wet vapour."

35

chamber like the Snow King's audience hall, another pearly one that must have been Venus's ballroom. In one of them rascally old Fitzcollop had been most troublesome on the occasion of the Prince's party; he must have been drunk, she supposed; the Russian cordials given in honour of the Emperor were very strong. But what did it all matter now? Perhaps she had been unwarrantably cruel. . . . She checked herself with horror; that old reprobate! Was she going mad in her last days? She caught sight of her face dimly reflected in one of the many bits of mirror with which the pearly walls were encrusted. It certainly showed something of a mad air. If old Fitzcollop with his senile lustings after housemaids and parsons' daughters could see her now, how ashamed he would be of those far-off protestations that had had nothing noble about them save their youth . . . .

Here, if she remembered rightly, there was an alcove with a fireplace and a sofa. Yes, all was still in place, though one twisted leg of the sofa was gone so that the whole lurched crazily like a wreck at low tide. With the stuffing that burst out of a dozen rents was mixed a mass of small shells, as fine as anemone petals, that had fallen from the overhanging stalactites; while fungus and a pallid sort of fern were creeping among the icicles and rustications of the fireplace. How long was it since a fire had danced there, its flames leaping up to meet some bright luxurious verse turned out in a wanton moment that must, she was sure, have brought remorse in its train? How long since the sofa bore some light and scandalous burden as the fire died?

"Easy, my Lady," Titmarsh was already in the bathroom, "easy, till I strikes a light; it be powerful dark here, to be sure."

In one of the sconces, made from coral branches and shells, there was still a candle, black and twisted, but good enough. It cast an unkind light upon the rents in the shell garlands, the medallions in spar that Tryphena's mother had prudently defaced before the Emperor's arrival. The original furniture had also been removed (rightly so, it was said). A disused garden roller, some flower-pots, a roll of bass and a rusty watering-can were at present the only equipment of this notorious apartment; one of the steps down into the bath was missing, while the yellowing tiles whereon La Fiorina's shameless form had reclined now bore nothing more wanton than last year's leaves.

36

"He were a rare one," Titmarsh chuckled, "your great-grandad, begging your Ladyship's pardon: a proper character, if ever there was; and that wild—wilder'n my little bitch June when she gets after a rabbit among the lettuces. Why, when I were a slip of a lad, no higher'n a raspberry cane, often's the day I'd hear old folk tell of his Lordship's queer ways and fancies. Proper madcap doings there were, from all they do say: foreign hussies running about the park of a summer evening dressed in next to nothing, an' excusing theirselves on account of it being so powerful hot. My old grandmum seed them with her own eyes, she did. Heat, she used to say; if there was real heat anywhere it were in their own shameless bodies, she said. But they was a fine well-made pack of wenches, every one of them, my old grandmum would give his Lordship that." Titmarsh smiled. "From all I've heard say, his Lordship, whatever his faults—and no disrespect meant, my Lady —his Lordship had a proper sharp eye for a pretty shape, that he had, and no mistake; and the properest man to make a garden too, when all's said. My grandad lived till ninety-two and knowed some'at of his trade; well, he'd allus say, he would, that nobody could match his Lordship when it came to gardening, and my grandad knowed a thing or two, as the saying is."

"Yes, Titmarsh, quite so." She began to retrace her steps out of the grotto; she had little mind to exchange this pearly illusion for the grey one of the mist, but she was growing cold; dank vapours were swirling down the long funnels that served as windows to the bathroom; they were forming into great drops on the ends of the stalactites, drops as still as the mist that had borne them, so still it seemed as if real stalactites of crystal were at last growing on to the man-made shell ones. The wet vapours were clutching at the candle-flame, making it dance for its life; they were trying to penetrate her pelisse, and set a whole complicated mechanism of pain to work in her throat and in her troublesome shoulders. Plummett would be for ever nagging and whining at her if she caught a chill here; at her age, to catch a chill from loitering in an old grotto!

"Come, Titmarsh, I've much to do this morning."

As if ignoring her excuse, "Yes, my Lady, a proper dank place it is," he said, "and wicked for the rheumatics; we'd best not linger."

As they returned by the spiral passages, Tryphena noticed a

"Come, Titmarsh, I've much to do this morning."

medallion with the design executed in small bright shells upon a background of the darkest spar; it depicted a horse of consummate grace and power; its noble head was embellished by a tall plume, upon its back was perched what Tryphena at first took for a jockey. But there was something not quite natural about the jockey's air. Tryphena, pulling a lorgnette from her reticule, looked closer. It was dark enough in this loop of the passage, so that for a moment she could distinguish nothing of the jockey's face. Then she discerned a forehead low even for a jockey, a face more wizened than anything she had ever seen on Newmarket Heath, a lower lip that jutted out in front as far as did the brim of the jockey cap itself. About the seat of the rider, the cast of his shoulders there was something—she did not precisely know what—something almost inhuman. She felt even colder than before.

"Titmarsh," she called. As usual, he was far ahead, at the door of the grotto. He never waited, but without hurrying, rather with the smooth progress of a clock, he would move from one point to another, not stopping for any trifle.

"Titmarsh!" once again; but he was already almost back at her side.

She pointed with her lorgnette to the medallion. "I've never seen that before; it only goes to show how little I use my eyes. But the jockey, Titmarsh—I declare I've rarely seen a droller figure; and the plume. One of my great-grandfather's favourite race-horses, I suppose. But why the plume?"

"That bain't no racehorse, not by a long way that bain't, begging your Ladyship's pardon. Don't your Ladyship know what that be?"

"I haven't the least idea." She spoke coldly, nettled by the thought of his superior knowledge.

"Why, Lord bless you, my Lady, did you never hear tell of your great-grandad's string of circus horses? How they was that clever they could drill like a pack of red-coats, and die for England when you mentioned it to them, and dance like the finest lady in the land, and walk like her too, on their hind legs, so natural, you'd never believe!"

Yes, now she recalled some stories of them, she could not quite say what. But four of their circus plumes had crowned the posts of the first proper bed she'd ever possessed. They were already a

39

trifle old and thin, the plumes, when she had them, but vastly grand and pretty, she had thought, in their pale pinks and greens. Though she had been but thirteen at the time, the sight of those tall and lovely plumes crowning her small bed had made her feel, she recalled, as if she were already a married lady with a pack of the prettiest and most tiresome children imaginable, to say nothing of her own carriage.

"Yes, yes," she snapped testily at him, furious at herself on account of the plumes. "Yes, of course, I've heard about the circus horses. My great-grandfather found them, I've been told, in Germany and was so catched by their pretty manners he bought them there and then at an immense price, for the circus had no thought or wish to part with them. Most extravagant and eccentric of his Lordship, but in keeping with all else he did, and no doubt they were very beguiling animals. Yes, of course, all that I know. But the jockey—explain me that, Titmarsh, just explain me that. A jockey on a circus horse; I've rarely encountered a stranger fancy."

"Jockey, jockey? Lord save me, my Lady, that bain't no jockey, that bain't. Oh no; no more'n what he's up on's a racehorse. No, indeed."

"Oh! for goodness sake come to the point. I'm far too busy to stand here all day catching my death and listening to you telling me what something isn't."

"Beg pardon, my Lady, beg pardon, I'm sure. If your Ladyship'll be pleased to leave this wet old place."

"But the jockey, the jockey!"

"Why that, my Lady, that's an ape or monkey, as the saying is."

"Monkey, ape; don't talk nonsense; apes don't ride horses, least of all rigged up as jockeys."

Titmarsh exasperatingly shook his head again. "That bain't no jockey's rig, my Lady."

"Titmarsh, if you say that bain't this or that to me again this morning I shall grow so mad I'll have one of my attacks of asthma. Answer me like the sensible man they hold you to be, not like a ninny!"

Titmarsh started to say "That bain't" once more, checked himself in time. Finally he said: "His Lordship used to put them circus horses to drive his *calèche*. The smartest turn-out you ever

40

did see, so I've heard. Shaped something like a shell, it were (his Lordship were always a proper one for shells, as this place testifies); it were as light and quick as a spring breeze. Well, he'd put his precious circus horses between the shafts, for he always did like to take the ribbons to a nice spirited team of cattle, as the saying is. But with them circus horses, there were just nothing in it; they was that clever, they knowed what he wanted afore he did hisself; and so, since his Lordship were allus a great one for fancy notions, he took some apes out of his menagerie and set 'em to ride on them there high-steppers, dressed as pos——" Searching for the word, Titmarsh twisted his three-cornered hat in tortures of not so much embarrassment as annoyance.

"Postillions is what you mean."

"Yes, my Lady, postillions them were." He smiled gratefully. "My old grandad used to tell me how when he were naught but a little lad he'd often seen his Lordship drive into Bearminster in his turn-out, a pack of foreign ladies with him as bold as brass, and them heathen monkeys riding pos——, riding postillion. The strangest sight it were, but a brave one too, when the turn-out dashes down the High Street, cross Cornmarket, making for the Assembly Rooms, with them horses curvetting ever so pretty, and them plumes tossing away, and them heathen apes screaming and chattering like a lot of clever demons. My Lord, I'd like to have seen it, just once like. He were a rare one, were his Lordship. They don't make 'em like that now, not by a long way, and that's the truth."

V

THE MIST HAD GROWN THICKER SINCE THE GROTTO had engulfed them; but it bothered Titmarsh little, for he exactly knew the disposition of every parterre and fountain, every temple and folly in the garden. He walked for a time in silence, a little ahead of her, on the very fringe of her vision. Then suddenly:

"They do say, my Lady, as them apes ride still; of a quiet night in summer, and even times when it's blowed in from the sea hard-like, there be some as swears to have seen them creatures riding like the Fiend hisself, lickety-spit across the park, screeching and whistling fit to raise the house; and the plumes tossing like mad things. That silly young Tim now; he do hold to have seen them one June evening a couple of years back, the night Lady Deborah had her bad attack, it were. But don't you take no notice of what that numskull says, my Lady. He be a terrible one for listening to silly women's tales, begging your Ladyship's pardon and no offence intended."

She was hardly listening; visions of wicked great-grandpapa Winterbourne and his strange doings obsessed her; upon that enigmatic figure Titmarsh had cast this morning almost a new light. To a certain degree, she realised, this wicked ancestor of hers had always fascinated her, at least whenever she had visited his garden. Yet, though every stone, every glade of Uptake told of him, she had never been able to garner many details about his life. Grandpapa Indus had died before her curiosity matured; her parents would hardly suffer the scandalous name to be mentioned. For them it was enough that the Reverend Mr. Hogburton down at the Rectory had been constrained publicly to pray for Lord Winterbourne's salvation; never more, the reverend gentleman announced, would he let his cloth darken the doors of Uptake. The fact that wicked great-grandpapa had not for years invited him to do so was, as her parents rightly said, not the point, though they owned that Mr. Hogburton had gone a little far when he refused a Viscount Christian burial. . . .

It was sad that great-grandpapa had been so wicked, for in his way he had been a man of parts. Had he not after all, just to show his mastery of all natural forces, transformed a desert of marsh and bare headlands into as fair an estate as you could see, draining the brackish pools, transplanting whole meadows of lush grass, even full-grown trees, from half across the kingdom, blocking the turn-pikes for days at a time with them; and setting them up with soft

"She was hardly listening."

grass around them and bright pheasants feeding on their nuts, where once a mournful gull or at most a curlew was to be seen?

Titmarsh of a sudden halted. "Hark, my Lady! I reckon there do be a horseman a-coming up of the drive."

At first Tryphena could hear nothing save the distant sea-birds, moisture falling on to sodden leaves, the squawk and flurry of a pheasant surprised by some terror out of the mist. Then she caught the remote echo of hooves, so muffled and twisted by the fog it was like a sound heard between sleeping and waking. For a moment, recalling Titmarsh's story, she had a fancy that the rider must be a monkey. Half laughing at herself, she reflected, really what a tiresome humour a slight thing like a misty morning had put her in. But her rally to reason was not lasting. The sound of the horseman died away, she thought no more of the monkey riders, yet the morning was now spoilt for her, the mist was filled with forebodings of some unknown mischief, that made her feel at one with the frightened pheasant.

To the left of where they were walking the ground rose steeply, falling away again to their right. They crossed a little stream that clattered fussily from one pool to another, down toward the invisible river. Titmarsh paused again.

"I've said before and, begging your Ladyship's pardon, I'll say again, what this garden needs to finish it off proper-like be a nice water-organ, like what plays in that there Austrian bishop's grounds; as sweet as a flute it were, and talked of for miles around. Now if we was to have one here at Uptake, no garden in the kingdom could come near us. It wouldn't cost more'n next to nothing, and here be the place made by the Lord hisself for it."

The water-organ. Why must Titmarsh mention that? The two words were like some witch's enchantment that set loose a pack of demons against her heart. To Tryphena they brought back with insupportable poignancy all the nightmare of Adolphus's death; for it was during the bringing home of the dear body from Greece that Titmarsh had first seen a water-organ—somewhere near Salzburg she believed; on his return he had talked of nothing else, thinking no doubt to distract her from her grief. No word about the final putting of Adolphus under Irish ground, at far-away Ballyfinnan; so far as she could recall he had rarely again mentioned Adolphus's name, though he had adored him; and he would never

44

say anything of the ghastly journey back, with those barbarous Irish drinking and roystering and brawling half across Europe, the dear coffin often lying abandoned in the foreign mud while these madmen broke heads and pillaged wine-shops, just because they could not make themselves understood.

Ballyfinnan had come to Adolphus through his mother; and he had always preferred it to Uptake, no doubt because it was his very own, while here he was merely the younger brother—at least so he would say, though Heaven knew poor Matthew had doted upon him, had asked nothing better than that Adolphus should never cease to consider the place as his home. But Adolphus had chosen to be an Irish squireen among his bogs and dream there of thyme-scented Grecian hills. Tryphena had never cared for Bally-finnan. The house itself was all very well, a typical Irish manor with neat bow-windows and a pediment big enough for a palace; about its ill-proportioned gentility there hung a rather endearing air; but the ruin down by the ford depressed her, that vast unfurnished shell, with windows unfilled and fireplaces that had always stood cold, a folly gaping roofless at the wet skies. An Earl of Amarys, one of her mother's ancestors, a proud and uncertain subject if ever there was one, had put his heart into the building of it. Then Queen Elizabeth, hearing of its tremendous walls, had hinted that the completion of it would be regarded as tantamount to high treason. Amarys had dismissed his masons, and as if life no longer held any purpose for him he died in the following winter. About the bones of his superb project there seemed to flit the ghost of a heart once proud, passionately calling the living to bear witness to the vanity of all human aims. The spectre of the broken-hearted Amarys and the sullen laughter of Adolphus's tenants had alike repelled Tryphena. Adolphus, however, had adored place and people, and vowed he would be buried nowhere but at Ballyfinnan.

Then, one day, disaster had arrived, in the shape of a wicked Epirote. Tryphena could recall the man's first appearance with the utmost clarity. The whole family, Adolphus too, were up in London at Winterbourne House for some balls and a political crisis. A stranger fantastically dressed had arrived asking for Adolphus. Adolphus had been closeted with him for hours, and suddenly emerged radiant, announcing that he could for the moment attend

45

no more balls, nor take up the expensive seat in the Commons that the family had reserved for him. The Epirote stranger possessed news bearing all the air of truth, and according to which the tomb of the great Alexander had been come upon in a cave half-way down a cliff in Epirus; after questioning the man closely Adolphus was satisfied that there was much in his story. They were off accordingly the following week to make what might well be the most important archæological discovery of the age.

With a low heart, or perhaps with no heart at all, she watched them go, the Epirote ridiculous in a new beaver hat that Adolphus had bought him as more appropriate for the journey than his native skull cap. That was the last she ever saw of Adolphus; in her heart she knew that it would be so; nevertheless her lack of surprise did not mitigate the agony she suffered when months later she learnt through the Governor of the Ionian Islands—a cousin of theirs on her mother's side—that Adolphus had been killed at the very climax of his search. When he had descended the cliff to within a few feet of his putative goal his rope had been severed—whether by a rock-edge or a knife nobody knew—and he had been dashed to death below.

And then the wake! They had discovered that Adolphus in a romantic moment before leaving England had drawn up a will, with instructions for the waking back of his body to Ballyfinnan from wherever he might die. The charge he entrusted to his dear people of Ballyfinnan. Tryphena had argued that so fantastic a provision could not be held to apply to a death in a land as remote as Greece; but Matthew, the head of the family, and Louisa, Adolphus's rather ordinary wife, maintained against her that, whatever the cost, Adolphus's last wishes must be obeyed. The result had been two years of worry and of expense that permanently crippled the family.

"Them Irish," Titmarsh suddenly burst out, in his maddening way sensing her thoughts, "them Irish bain't nothing but a pack of shabby rascals; they bain't worth the decent potatoes they're raised on, as the saying is. Give me a proper foreigner any day. Leastways, if he does say the heathen things them Irish does, you can't understand him rightly. I were truly sorrowful for his poor Lordship, what with him perishing like that in his prime, far from his loved ones, but it were nothing to what them Irish made me go through on the journey back. No indeed! After all these years, I still wake up of nights in a muck sweat, a-thinking of their doings."

A representative section of Ballyfinnan citizens, the worst drunkards and bullies of the place, or so it seemed, had been shipped to Epirus, at unbelievable expense. Expense! It had only begun there. The bringing back of the dear remains which should have been a pious care, swiftly executed, had in fact become a drunken riot lasting two years. Titmarsh who had gone with the mourners to keep an eye on his late young master's coffin was powerless to check the disgraceful events that had marked Adolphus's last journey across Europe, and which had landed the Caudle family in ruinous litigation with half a dozen governments.

Titmarsh evidently had the affair on his mind; never, so far as Tryphena could recall, had he mentioned it to her before; but now he began to speak of it again, as if moved by her own preoccupation. "It were the biddies, as they calls 'em, as was the worst. Of a night, when we stopped in some little town, they'd start what they calls their keening outside the church where his poor Lordship had been put to lie. Lord grant that such a heathen clamour bain't never heard in Christian Uptake. Then the Paddies would eat and drink for an army, and start throwing the people of the place, what 'ud be sipping their pot of wine as quiet and moderate as you could want, into the fountains, and the biddies egging 'em on like a lot of crazy witches. Lord save us, if it hadn't been for a garden or two I seed, as fine and neatly ordered as anybody could think of, I reckon I should a been out of my mind afore we reached France."

All this, she thought bitterly, was nothing to the worries and humiliations that had been brought upon her by the whole episode. That ghastly reception at Devonshire House—she could recall it all too clearly—when the Foreign Secretary, whom her father had created, and into whose hair as a child she had twined many a daffodil garland, had almost ignored her, and had then complained with all the coldness upon which his parliamentary reputation was based, that the Caudles in their pride were allowing a matter of family obsequies to endanger the kingdom's good relations with half Europe. Such vanity, such arrogance, he had hinted, recalled the aristocratic disloyalty which, one hoped, had ended with the Wars of the Roses. The Right Honourable Gentleman prided himself upon being something of an historian; had he not written a

47

novel on the Little Princes in the Tower that had been well received by the *Quarterly Review?* . . . Then there were those never-ending bills, for pillagings, desecrations, incendiarism, the deflowering of even quite elderly nuns. . . . The list of crimes was as unending as the claims. Though it had all happened years ago, only last week Tryphena had paid out a large sum in compensation for the defiling, in a curious and licentious manner, of a holy water stoop at Innsbruck. And to think that these barbarians called themselves Catholics. . . .

It was terrible to think of the alleys neglected, the fences left to rot, in consequence of this mad and interminable expense. How poor Adolphus would have grieved to see Uptake dying from the corruption he was normally heir to and which had almost been transformed to the place from his embalmed body. He who had always worshipped life as a god, who could banish death even from the obscure questions, two thousand years and more in the grave, that it was his passion to study.

Just before you reached the pavilion that housed the Dancers you passed through a circular sort of glade. It was the only personal monument remaining at Uptake to the poor rich Miss Bouncer; a cemetery for the innumerable dogs and cats who had solaced her neglected existence—Brisks and Frisks and Selimas and Cæsars, to say nothing of a few elderly apes, with names like Marlborough, Loyal Tim, Orinooco, and Pliny.

Casting an eye upon the glistening tombstones, Titmarsh chuckled. "A proper rum lot we's always been at Uptake, and no mistake! There bain't been a day, I reckon, since Uptake was builded, but we've done something what most people never had the sense to think of!"

Sense! He seemed almost proud of all the Caudle extravagances. Perhaps, Tryphena reflected self-examining, perhaps she was guilty of an equal folly. Yet in her heart of hearts she knew that by all proper standards it was a vain and lamentable pride that all unknowing gloried in its own ruin. A house, a dynasty could stand a proper constituent of eccentricity like the true proportion of yeast in a loaf. An extravagance of mind, if restrained to wise limits, was doubtless a good seasoning for a family's character, but with the Caudles you could not be sure that the seasoning had not outweighed every other element.

48

"Yes, Titmarsh, most people would say we're strange enough. There's been hardly a generation till our time that has not had its own peculiarities. My great-grandfather with his monkeys and circus horses; my grandmother here with her lavish tombs for pets, her commissioning of the most distinguished poets of the day to write the funeral orations for these animals; my grandfather conquering a vast empire by means of a frivolous and somewhat inhumane joke; Lord Adolphus losing his valuable life on a madcap quest; his late Lordship dying in Spain for a political cause that was in no way his, saying he was fighting for liberty, when he knew even less of what liberty is than I do."

"Truly said, your Ladyship, true enough. And what about your father, with all due respect to his Lordship; a better man never sat in the seats of the mighty and told the foreigner just because he lives in a nice place it don't entitle him to speak about what he don't know nothing of. I've read every speech his Lordship made; never man made wiser. Yet even his Lordship as we all well know had his fads; leeks he couldn't abide in his garden; scratch away like a mad cat he would if there was so much'n smell of them about the place.

"Titmarsh, he'd cry, Titmarsh, some rascally Taffy's been here, scattering his damned weed about the place. I won't have it, d'you see, I positively won't have it. Oh! terrible times I've had with him. Then there were the to-do about the choir."

Yes, Tryphena remembered that. An ardent churchgoer, her father had been profoundly shocked, on coming into Uptake, to learn that for miles around there was not a single church where the performance of the choir was much above the mutter of a herd of swine. Determined to correct this lamentable situation, he had assembled and personally trained a choir of remarkable quality, which he kept at Uptake all the year round, even when politics prevented him from leaving London for weeks at a time. During the periods of his living at Uptake the choir would constantly drill; then when Sunday came they would be packed into a vast sort of brake, whisked at a hand-gallop to some church where the vileness of the singing was notorious. Led by Tryphena's father they would slip discreetly into the back of the church and stay silent for a while. Then the moment for some hymn would arrive; the local choristers would rise with a great hollow clatter, wiping back the

49

"Then they were absorbed in their dance."

strands of vainly tallowed hair that invaded their hymn-books, opening their great mouths early as if to forestall any surprise attack by the music; there would be a wheezing and a rumble as the vicar's groom fell to the bellows; a few quavering notes pulled out of the machine by the vicar's ailing wife, and the yokels would suck in their breath for the first bawl. But hark! what was that? Instead of the cacophony that habitually deranged even the decorations for the Harvest Festival, a voice remote and disconcerting as the Phœnix would flutter among the still angels on the roof. The yowling of the clodhoppers would lose even its original semblance of order; the squire dozing in the secrecy of his high-walled pew would wake, snorting, "Damme, what's that namby-pamby row? Sounds devilish like one of those foreign operas"; the parson's wife, brooding at the organ, would be jerked out of her meditations upon Martha the cook and her wilfulness with quince jelly.

Then quietly Tryphena's father would carry his accomplished band out again leaving the congregation to a deserved shame and confusion. There would be another gallop in the swaying brake, another humiliation for a tasteless parish, till for miles around not a church but wore out its bovine choristers with practice, and then practice again, to guard against the terrible visitations from Uptake. . . .

Tryphena's mother, it was true, had on the whole been normal enough; her constant preoccupation with her health had left her little time for fancies. All the same, toward the end her behaviour had touched the extravagant; she had taken against her fond spaniel, Cicero, because he wouldn't whistle, even when she played upon the harp and bribed him with the best of gooseberries. She had, too, imagined that two hundred and sixty-nine bloodthirsty and licentious Frenchmen lurked to pounce upon her from the ambush of her sponge; in vain she had been reminded that France was respectable again, and our good friend; for all that, so long as she was living, nobody at Uptake might possess a sponge or speak French.

"Here be the Dancers' Pavilion," called Titmarsh, lost in the mist, "neater than whatever it's looked in our time, though I beg leave to say it."

Certainly the little temple was miraculously spick and span; the glass floor shone for once clear of leaves; the mirrored walls were no longer fly-blown, nor encrusted with cobwebs. Tryphena paid but the scantiest heed. She was still musing with almost horrified pride upon the Caudles and their queer ways. Matthew, for instance, dear, kind Matthew, whom she had never really bothered to value, Matthew dying in Spain, in a war that in no degree concerned him, for an ideal which, she suspected, he had but imperfectly understood . . . Deborah lost in a welter of prescriptions and physics; wicked young Henry with his incendiary mania. The barns and charred ricks that had been the victims of his dangerous folly; the shameful occasion when he had poured some pitch-like substance upon FitzCollop's moat at Pinmoney and had set fire to it in an effort, as he had lamely explained, to rid the walls of their picturesque foliage; his attempt to justify his evil act by describing the gorgeous old ivy as a suffocation had been voted empty frivolity worsened by bad taste. . . . Deborah and she had hardly felt justified in showing their heads outside Uptake all that summer. . . .

There began a whirring and a clicking; a hidden pipe-organ coughed twice and fell into an air of such unexpected vitality Tryphena almost jumped. A mirrored door came slowly open! Through it there tripped with a stiffness scarce perceptible the Dancers, restored to their former excellence and with a very smart appearance despite their old-fashioned dress. They were truly lifelike, Tryphena thought, as the gallant jerked a bow and his ballerina dipped a curtsy to her. Then they were absorbed in their dance, executing it with the utmost neatness; occasionally, it is true, a pale hand would tremble when extended in a gesture of respect, or there would come a slight creaking protest as the ballerina lowered her modest gaze; it was strange to come upon these tokens, as it were, of old age in creatures of an aspect so perennially young. . . .

VI

SUDDENLY THERE WERE HEARD STEPS UPON THE wet flags outside; Albert, the footman, stood before her. The wet had played the drollest tricks with his curls; they now seemed the most sodden thing in Uptake.

"Can't you see as her Ladyship be busy?" Titmarsh roared from some hiding-place in the organ.

"Very sorry, my Lady, I'm sure. But Lady Deborah asks will you go to her with all possible despatch?"

"What in Heaven can the matter be?"

"Her Ladyship just declared it was most urgent."

"Oh well, I suppose I must."

At that Titmarsh emerged from the organ, glaring at Albert. The Dancers had stopped.

"As pretty a job we've made of them as ever anyone seed; and your Ladyship will own as much."

"Indeed I do, indeed yes."

"Well, my Lady," he began, twisting his hat ominously.

"Yes, Titmarsh, what is it?"

"It's that there Philosopher."

The Sage. He lived in a cave down by the lake; originally, when you entered his abode he would rise from his apparent meditations and strike you gently with his stick, in token of your own worthlessness. He had been disconnected long ago, in Tryphena's childhood, for frightening some old aunt. Now, if you paid him a visit he no longer rose; he just glared.

"Well, what of it?" She was already making down the steps.

"I were just a-thinking, my Lady." He paused.

"What, Titmarsh, what, pray? You see that I'm in a hurry."

Indeed, Albert had already opened an umbrella, was spinning it about petulantly.

"I were just a-thinking as we might fix up the Philosopher proper-like, seeing as how we did such a fine job of the Dancers."

"But, Titmarsh, you know perfectly well that my father gave

53

particular orders against ever putting the Philosopher to rights again."

"But who's he to scare nowadays, a poor old doll like, even if he be a man's size. 'Twould surely take more'n that to scare your Ladyship, that it would."

"Oh well," she hesitated.

Albert coughed.

"Lady Deborah was very urgent on seeing your Ladyship without delay."

Tightening her fur cape about her she started back towards the house. The mist had developed into a sort of fine drizzle that assailed you from every hand, so that Albert's umbrella served no very good purpose. The most familiar thing, yew-trees, the little theatre where they used to act pieces of dear Adolphus's invention, all were distorted into fantastic shapes that set her thinking once again of the Caudle eccentricities. They were indeed a queer lot, fatally strange, even. It was a wonder that they had not brought disaster upon themselves.

When she came to think of it, she was the only one of the family who had never behaved in an extravagant or unreasonable manner. The reflection provoked in her a certain pride, with which a touch of something almost akin to disappointment was imperceptibly blended. Only her good head, she told herself, had kept Uptake together.

Then she suddenly thought of Lucius. Dear Lucius. He was sane and sensible enough, too. Lovely Uptake could be entrusted without fear to him. If only he were here now, the owner of the place, instead of being far off in Italy. When he had entered diplomacy, Tryphena's pleasure had been endless, he had seemed designed by the Fates for his calling, with his elegant manners, something of his father's heavenly looks, much, too, of his father's parts, without that fatal impetuosity. Tryphena sighed.

How long it was since she had last laid eyes on Lucius; eighteen months back lay that charming summer, when she had visited him. They had met in Milan and gone on together to Parma, where he was British Minister. She had been made an inordinate fuss of by the little gimcrack Court; they had even arranged a special theatrical performance in her honour, throwing open the theatre attached to the palace, a famous place in its time she'd heard, but

54

grown a trifle shabby of late. Still, the decoration was very hand-some, she had to allow, with the great wooden curtains restrained by Cupids and the richly gilt boxes. Then there had been music until past midnight on the silver-pink piazza, delicious white truffles and crayfish to eat, a vastly fine ceiling in the cathedral by Correggio—or was it Carpaccio? All painters' names confused her old head abominably—above all, when Lucius had carried her off to Venetia. They had stayed in an elegant villa, rather like Uptake, on a river between Padua and the sea; it had been the season of summer holidays or *villeggiatura,* when all the most distinguished Venetians moved out there, and the company had been very genteel. Apparently with the recent troubles, and the recent taste for mountains, this pleasant fashion was growing yearly less current; even Lucius, who loved the country, knowing by heart all the names of those important fresco painters who to a man had been christened Battista, even Lucius had not gone to Venetia last summer.

Dear, dear Lucius; she could see him now, leaning elegantly against a column in the guttering candle-light, staring with his incessant and fashionable melancholy toward the lights of Venice; while the vegetable boats drifted by to songs which sounded pretty enough, provided you didn't understand them, or a nobleman's barge would scrape through the lock with a great flourish of gilt and oaths and violins. Ah! Lucius back again; that would bring her peace, as if her darling Adolphus walked once more, an Adolphus in whose hands Uptake would be safe; she prayed that Lucius would marry well as he had always promised.

It was incredibly still within the house, after the chatter of wet upon a million leaves. Here and there the gas had been lit against the gloom, though it was no more than a few minutes past midday. In the Etruscan hall Hake popped from behind a great black vase.

"Lady Deborah wants to see your Ladyship quick. She said it would brook no delay."

"Very well, Hake." Tryphena hurried by. Albert disappeared, no doubt to neglect his duties and torture the housemaids.

To reach Deborah's room, you went through the Chinese state bedroom, a Chinese saloon, and then the Blue Drawing-room. Tryphena could never pass the Chinese state bed without a feeling

55

of mingled awe and pleasure; it was a contrivance of such exceptional nobility and imagination, with posts fashioned like tropic trees and a whole menagerie of hoopoes and devilish dragons on the top. Years ago a German prince, blessed with a consort of renowned ugliness, had paid a visit to Uptake and had been put to lie in this bed. It was reported that his Grand Ducal Highness, waking in the dawn and discerning through the grey light the outline of some ferocious form that grinned at him from the bed-top, had uttered a wild shriek: "Augusta, Augusta!" he had roared. "Je te supplie, mein schatz! Kom' sofort en bas! E finita la commedia! Es schmerzt mich inniglich dass ich dich offensiert habe!"

What was now the Blue Drawing-room had once been Chinese also; but the bamboos and the birds of longevity had been discoloured by a burst pipe; so a flock paper in a handsome Prussian blue had taken their place. Lucius always complained of it as an error of taste, but then he was strangely conservative for someone who was only forty. To Tryphena's eye, the blue was a happy innovation; the gilt mirrors with their icicles and windmills and donkeys glowed as never they did in the days of the Chinese paper. When the time came to die, Tryphena thought, she would choose if she could to walk up one of those flights of gilt steps, under a ruined arch, losing herself in the glassy pool that the gilt rocks kept free of all wind. . . .

Deborah's maid, Drax, a flag-pole if ever there was one, met her in the library.

"Her Ladyship," she murmured severely, "is in a terrible perturbation; she's been asking for *your* Ladyship this full hour; I've been hard put to know what to say."

Another of Deborah's attacks, Tryphena gloomily imagined. There was something pontifical about dear Deborah's attacks. They were her vocation: when one of them was brewing it was as if Lord Byron were busy upon an ode, or some great composer after sterile weeks had been glimpsed moving restlessly toward his pianoforte. All Uptake bated its breath, until the Doctor emerged from the sickroom. He would invariably trip down the great stairs in silence, nor would he break it too soon. He would jump into his gig, his cattle would stamp and toss their heads impatiently: "Easy there, easy, my fine beauties". Then as the pink-and-blue rug was wrapped round him and he stretched toward the whip he would toss a word to the waiting Hake: "We're a trifle easier this morning; we're down to a fraction over a hundred and one; it was no doubt the ointment that relieved us." Or: "We passed a somewhat restless night, Hake"; a shake of the head: "but let there be no vexing of the spirit. It is all in the hands of the Lord and He in His mercy will heal us, what with some judicious cupping, and a posset we've prescribed, of eggs beaten up with a pinch of nutmeg, black pepper, and a good lashing of Hungarian Tokay."

The words would be echoed down the bright corridors with eager commentaries; there would be a sense of some problem resolved, as if the poet had at last found the happy conceit to fit the forest fire, or the scherzo no longer trailed off unfinished into the impatient air.

Tryphena checked her thoughts guiltily. What a malicious old woman she was becoming! But then, had she not some right to her thoughts when she had given up her life, since darling Adolphus's

" . . . losing herself in the glassy pool that the gilt rocks kept free of all wind."

57

death at least, to the tending of poor Deborah? Nobody would ever know what an effort it had cost, the unreasoning distaste with which the very thought of ill-health inspired her. Nobody would know; to the County, for instance, she was, she had heard, a model of sisterly affection; it was wonderful, they said, that she and Deborah had each other; and, indeed, life would be unthinkable without her sister; the constant titillation of the protective impulse, the apotheosis earned by long smoothings of a fevered brow, the smile of gratitude as wan and precious as a Christmas sun. The bookcase was filled with learned reports upon the disease to which poor Deborah was particularly prone; some of them were quite modern and Deborah had contracted them before anybody else in the kingdom. In the corner of the room stood the massive handsome piece of luggage that enshrined Deborah's prescriptions, thousand upon thousand of them, Tryphena believed; ranged and indexed with the utmost neatness, they travelled with Deborah whithersoever she went, to London, Bath, Brighton, Malvern, Spa, Baden-Baden, and the lesser places where you took the waters. . . .

VI

WHEN SHE ENTERED THE BEDROOM TRYPHENA was surprised by the absence of all medicinal reek; indeed, for once there was no panoply of sickness at all, no drawn blinds nor steaming kettles, no mustard plasters nor measuring glasses; while Deborah—whom she had expected to find in bed, clutching painfully at her sweat-soaked sheets—Deborah was up, seated at her rosewood davenport, bent over innumerable packets of letters. In contrast to Tryphena, who could hardly bring herself to write two lines to a tenant for fear lest her precious daydreams might be shattered, Deborah was a loyal and industrious correspondent. What spare time her ill-health left her was spent in the exchange of intelligence with her score of relatives that were scattered about Europe and with her friends. The letters, invariably indited in neat and noble hands, were rarely thrown away; ranged as carefully as if they had been prescriptions, they were kept for the current year in the davenport and then at the New Year stacked in the upper shelves of the aromatic cupboards, above the ball-dresses of every sort, from the richest brocades to the Indian muslins, that long ago had shown off Deborah's pretty figure. (The to-do there had been when Deborah had damped the muslin so that it clung to her in a way that suggested some loose woman in France!)

All the packets of letters had been turned out, even from the cupboards, so that a faint scent of lavender, rather than of medicine, hung in the still air. Deborah always turned out her letters when she was upset. Was she going to contract one of her nervous attacks this time?

"Good morning, dear sister. Isn't the weather wretched? And I'm truly vexed to hear that you passed an uncomfortable night."

Tryphena bent and kissed the still pretty brow. She was reassured by its coolness.

Deborah raised her eyes to her sister; in their time those eyes had been famous for their lustre; now they were dull, the lids swollen and red.

"What! Tears? Dearest Deborah, what is it? Tell me, I pray you!"

Deborah clutched her sister's hand, began to tremble, as the tears rose again in her.

"Ah no! My precious sister, you mustn't cry, positively you mustn't. What in Heaven's amiss?"

For a time Deborah could not speak for the sobs that shook her. Tryphena began to lose patience; no doubt it was little but some silly fancy, the thought of being a lonely old maid perhaps. She sighed.

The sobs were ebbing now, had died away. Deborah was staring at her. Suddenly she spoke, hardly above a whisper:

"He's dead; I've just had intelligence."

"Who?" But Tryphena already half guessed; with a chilling heart she recalled the sound of the hurrying courier in the misty drive. "Is it poor darling Lucius?" It was a certain relief to pronounce the name.

Deborah nodded. "He caught fever down in some forsaken part of the Maremma. There's a long letter of regret from the Foreign Office."

The Foreign Office! A skein of memories was invoked by those two words to entangle her heart: her father with his red boxes and

59

all the parade of international conferences; Lucius as a young gentleman there flirting with the pretty milliners across the narrow street, by means of a mirror and the sun. . . .

"What," Tryphena asked dully, "what was he about in those parts—they can have no diplomatic importance?"

"He was on some archæological pursuit concerned with the Etruscans."

Archæology. The parallel between Lucius and his darling father was too close. Tryphena closed her eyes, as if to shut out the pitiless mist.

"Why, oh why, must archæology kill them both?" she whispered; "after all, what is it but a distraction for gentlemen of taste; and yet it's taken Adolphus and now Lucius from us as if they were mere nobodies."

It now fell to Deborah to comfort. "There, there," she whispered. "I gather he felt no pain, perceived not at all how hopeless it all was."

But Tryphena could not listen; she was rocking to and fro, like any new widow on her cottage doorstep, crying:

"What will become of us now? Who is to care for my lovely Uptake? He was so handsome, and generous, and a radiant smile for everybody; they would have doted upon him to folly here. Oh, my poor, poor little Lucius! It seems but yesterday we were sending you back in the old coach to catch the stage for Eton. . . . We were so proud of him, Deborah, weren't we? We dreamed of Uptake cherished and handed on from one age to another, and now there remains nobody to hand it on to."

Deborah was for a time silent—she was smoothing Tryphena's hair with a tenderness that was at once surprising and a trifle disconcerting in her who throughout life had remained prettily indifferent to all but her own immediate suffering.

"There, there, dear sister; Lucius loved you; you were his favourite aunt; and you know how much I loved him. Only once before has there been such a calamity fall upon us." She gazed curiously at Tryphena. "You know what I mean."

Tryphena did know. She fell to sobbing once more.

"There's still poor Henry, remember."

"Impossible, quite impossible. That blackguard! Deborah, I'm truly surprised at you."

60

"But he's the last male Caudle."

"There's always Septimus Caudle."

"That unctuous colonial parson? To begin with, he's not descended from wicked great-grandfather, as you know well; and therefore he can lay no claim either to the Marquisate or to our dear Uptake. The Winterbourne Viscountcy would, I suppose, go to him, and that would already be far too much for a parson of so little consequence. No, he must be left to do what he's pleased to call his invaluable work upon that Australian sheep station with the barbarous name—Walla, Walla something, ain't it called?"

"Wallaballoo, you mean." The outlandish sound of the name set Tryphena sniffing faintly with distaste.

Deborah, too, wrinkled her fine nose. How lucky her sister had been, Tryphena thought enviously, to have escaped the family beak.

"Wallaballoo. Yes, that was it. Wallaballoo. Just imagine the disposition of a man, even if he does happen to be a Minister of God, who could live in a place with a name like that!"

The thought of anything at once so horrible and so ridiculous as somebody from Wallaballoo laying claim to Uptake for a moment roused the sisters from their despair. Into Tryphena's tear-stained vision there began to swing back the ordinary objects that furnished the room, the engravings of *Les Femmes Savantes*, and of the *Promenade au Bois de Boulogne:* the draped dressing-table that always had about it somewhat the air of an overdressed cat: the swan-headed curtain poles. It was impossible, impious even, for them to look unchanged by darling Lucius's death; monstrous that the parrot Hasdrubal should continue quietly his sideway dances, croaking as he did so his usual chant, "Wilkes and Liberty; Wilkes and Liberty"; or, very occasionally, "My Lords and Turkeycocks . . ."

"Come," whispered Deborah suddenly, dabbing at her eyes, "come, let's go out and take a turn. I suffocate here."

"But the mist? Your poor chest?"

"Much does my wretched chest matter now. Come!"

She rose, smoothing down her stiff satins with a faint rustle that recalled the sea over the hill. Across the stricken face there fled the faintest smile.

61

"Amid all this calamity, I forgot to tell you, my dear, that there's a letter from Aunt Lavinia Bubikov. She's vastly vexed that we forgot her eighty-ninth birthday; she writes in a very bad humour indeed." Deborah paused. "I have an idea her temper has not been improved by the misfortune that's lately afflicted the Bubikovs."

"What misfortune? I've heard nothing."

"But that Nicky's duel, of course. He nearly killed some Grand Duke."

"Over a strumpet, I suppose?"

"No. A dog. What in Russia they call a borzoi. They use them for hunting the wolf. There was, it would seem, a bet that ended in Nicky's brute taking his Imperial Highness for the quarry. A challenge naturally followed, Nicky unfortunately triumphed and has been exiled to Piatigorsk in the south, to take the waters for two years; he has, of course, you'll remember, a property there. As a devoted mother, Aunt Lavinia has thought it prudent to follow her darling, and they live in a welter of insane quarrelling, which is not in any way relieved by her regrets for a lost Petersburg season. To read her lamentations on that account, you might think her a chit of twenty."

For a moment Tryphena almost forgot her grief. No intelligence about Aunt Lavinia and the Bubikov family had yet failed to divert her. Years ago, almost before Tryphena was born, Aunt Lavinia, the prettiest of the first Marquess's pretty, affected daughters, had bestowed her graceful person and her over-richness of sensibility in marriage upon a Russian, Prince Bubikov. It was at the time considered a brilliant match. The bridegroom was possessed of legendary wealth; he enjoyed the revenues of the vodka monopolies from the Governments of Perm, and Kertch, and Tula, treasures that had been imperially bestowed upon his father as a tribute to his virility. Prospects of almost oriental splendour had opened before the romantic Lavinia Caudle, estates over which you could ride for two days without reaching their boundaries, villages of dwarfs, Chinese and monkeys, jewels as large and rare as phœnix eggs, a bright blue Italian palace in Petersburg that contained a ballroom for one thousand dancers and walls of choice amber. Nor were any of these reports exaggerated. The young English bride found that it took nearer three days than

62

two to cross each Bubikov estate, the villages housed more dwarfs and Chinese than she had ever thought of, the ballroom could engulf fifteen hundred guests, the jewels had been so magnificent she could hardly move beneath their weight.

But Prince Bubikov had early proved very difficult, if not downright eccentric. To begin with, he was so addicted to horse-flesh and the saddle he would remain on horseback even indoors. Then he quickly betrayed an inordinate jealousy, that was apparently fed by malicious gossip from London on Lavinia's behaviour there as a débutante. He forbade her all commerce with the young blades of the capital; next, he denied her even female company, lest wanton intelligence might reach her thereby. Disaster was the only fruit of this harshness. Riding home one day, when his Lavinia had just begun her first pregnancy, the Prince noticed that his stirrup was taken by the second instead of the first footman. He enquired where the first one was, an unusually handsome lad. Igor Nicholaivitch, it seemed, was missing from the pantry, had not been seen for a full half-hour, not in fact since the Princess had rung for him.

With a wild cry, the Prince clapped spurs to his English hunter, galloped up the great marble stairway, cantered at the tall door of the nuptial chamber. Lavinia was sunk in the most agreeable of reveries when the door was burst open and a vicious equine head, with ears flattened angrily back, and a display of huge discoloured teeth, entered her voluptuous vision. From this apparition had come a bad-tempered whinny; Lavinia straightway fainted; on the strength of the whinny and her fainting, the Prince had taken Lavinia's guilt as proven, but in a drinking bout with the gipsies "to forget" he had suddenly been brought low with apoplexy. At eight months Lavinia had given birth to Cousin Nicky, whose appearance from the first provoked some misgiving; when he was no more than two years old his baby teeth were larger than a grown man's; the upper lip was of prodigious length, the nostrils and ears flattened wickedly back. The speech which he tardily acquired possessed a disturbing quality as of whinnying that his rare laughter served if anything to enhance. Growing up to his rightful wealth and honours he had contrived to be accepted in Russia as a person too distinguished to be judged by normal standards of appearance; but when he came to England in the

63

Emperor's train, and was summoned to Carlton House, the Prince took one horrified look at him, and then "Lord save us all," he cried, "is this pretty Lavinia Caudle's boy? Why, gentlemen, there's but one thing to be done. Let's put him to a brood mare, and run the issue at Newmarket."

With the years, the extravagance of poor Aunt Lavinia's

"Lavinia . . . had fallen into a fit of the sulks."

behaviour had grown. On her visits to England she complained that there were not enough servants at Uptake, and flew into a rage if everybody in the countryside didn't doff their hats or curtsy to her. For all that she preserved a touching affection for the place and for her relatives; at the New Year she never failed to send a splendid present. These presents, that at first had been of normal size, had, when she attained a valiant fifty, begun to grow in bulk and importance. Exquisitely painted sleighs, that might some day come in handy, had been succeeded by vases of lapis-lazuli, each one of which could secrete three men and cause the drawing-room floor ominously to sag. There were half a dozen of them, that grew steadily in size up to the latest monster. No present, you would have thought, could well be larger. But one year there had been received at Uptake news of a gift from Aunt Lavinia in ten crates so bulky they must be floated up the river in two barges. The crates unpacked had revealed a complete malachite staircase for Uptake; not a main staircase but an important one.

Aunt Lavinia in her redoubtable person was due to visit Uptake the following summer; so, to avoid unpleasantness, it was decided to install the staircase without delay. The operation had entailed vast and costly alterations that had been hardly completed by the time of her arrival; indeed, when tripping down her latest present in the dark, she had tripped over a painter's bucket, and bruised herself in a place less dignified than painful. She had taken her mishap badly; being now entirely Russified, she had demanded that the offending painter be thrashed to death. For the sake of peace, dear Matthew had affected to approve this punishment; when Lavinia a few days later had come upon the painter blithely whistling on a ladder, she had fallen into a fit of the sulks that had carried her away from Uptake six weeks before the intended close of her visit. Next year the present had been nothing more than a meagre fur rug. . . .

As now with Deborah she descended the famous staircase Tryphena reflected how invincibly garish it still contrived to appear.

"All the same," said Deborah, reading her thoughts, "this is what the sight-seers like, more than anything in Uptake."

They began almost to laugh; then at the turn of the stairs they came suddenly upon a sketch of poor darling Lucius, done years

65

ago when he was a royal page. The sight of him, in his pretty clothes and boyish curls, looking like the radiant ghost of his father, was too much. The tears came on again, hotter, more hopeless than ever.

The mist had lifted a bit and drawn back from the sun; the sun was white and weak like something that had lived for ever underground. But why complain of the sun? Tryphena bitterly reflected. Why complain of anything now that all your hopes are dead? For three decades she had wished Lucius were her child. Now for the first time she was thankful to have been spared that additional pang.

But when, as they walked in the wet park, they looked back at the great house, saw it gleaming wetly in the slackening embrace of the mist, a rock of richest quartz shining in an unknown valley, Tryphena suddenly said:

"Dear sister, you are right. Henry, for all his wickedness, must come back; there must be new life here."

There was no answer from Deborah. Tryphena looked at her, could almost have screamed in exasperation. Deborah had suddenly returned to her old tricks, withdrawn into the selfish fortress of ill-health; small beads of sweat were gathering upon the once crystal brow; the breathing grew laboured; Deborah leaned for a moment against a sphinx; then without a word went in to her stuffy room.

VII

FOR DAYS, AS THE MIST CLOSED ONCE MORE ABOUT the house, Tryphena struggled to obtain agreement from her sister upon Henry's return. But Deborah, who had first advocated it, could now caught in the ritual of her disorders spare no time to give further thought to the matter. From behind a barricade of doctors and physics, she would entreat that no agitating thought be permitted to upset her. Tryphena could act as she thought best. . . .

Desperately Tryphena might argue an injustice had been done. The wretched Henry, however worthless, had only stolen what now

66

they knew was rightfully his; they must never forget his claim as head of the family to Uptake; Henry's follies were but those of unprincipled youth. . . .

"Do as you please," Deborah would faintly answer, and prepare herself to receive the doctor.

One night Tryphena dreamed she saw before her a hand with at first many fingers upon it. But little by little their number dwindled till there were only three left; suddenly mouths began to grow upon these; the fingers fell to arguing, shrieking and abusing each other; the nails grew suffused with angry blood, the joints swelled with rage. At last the warring fingers bit each other off, so that at the end there was nothing left but a silly hand with a mass of bleeding stumps.

Much distressed, she went to Deborah early next morning, recounted the dream to her. "It's a plain sign, dear sister, a sign from on high to call Henry back. We must hope if we do so we shall find that exile has cleansed his heart of wickedness and that he will henceforward be tender of the family honour."

"I too have dreamed about it. Indeed, in one of my most recent dreams I saw poor Henry."

"You actually saw him? How did he appear?"

"He was standing on a sort of stone causeway; it was foggy, and from somewhere invisible came the sound of a horrible garish music; in those pale blue eyes of his there was an expression of ineffable sadness and he seemed very wet; water was dripping from the brim of his beaver and forming in great drops upon his poor weak chin. He pulled his watch out; it had stopped, I saw, at twenty-five past two; from his watch-pocket gushed a small torrent."

"You know, dearest Deborah," Tryphena seized her hand, "we did what we thought right at the time, both for the family honour and his regiment's, but we've been aware now long enough that we and his colonel were all mistaken. We ought to have brought him back long ago and cleared his name."

"But his intention was evil. He did not know, he probably still has no inkling, that the jewels he stole to pay that wretched debt were not ours but his. After all we didn't know, until those horrible solicitors discovered the codicil."

"Nevertheless, we realise now he was wrongfully put out of the

Army and of this country. Uptake is properly his and he must be brought back to it, particularly now he is the last of us. We must swallow our wicked pride and bring him back, so that he may marry suitably and beget heirs for Uptake."

Deborah pointed out with some reason that Henry had never been known to devote a minute of his attention to any female who might remotely be described as suitable; nevertheless, she agreed he must be induced to return.

When they had written to their cousin at the Washington Legation, invoking help for the finding of Henry without delay, it was at once as if a shameful obscurity had been lifted from off their minds. The seasons seemed to give sanction to their act; the seemingly eternal mist lifted once again from off the sodden ground, to disclose a few furtive snowdrops. Deborah almost disregarded her maladies, and took frequent turns with her sister through the grounds, discussing this and that future improvement. It would be spring before Henry could be back, even if his whereabouts were immediately discovered.

There was much work to be done in the gardens against his return. The sisters no longer remembered Henry's hatred for everything rural save the racecourse and the low tavern; they assumed without hesitation that in his rebirth he would prove himself a model landlord; and while they were upset by the way in which Titmarsh and that good-for-nothing Tim as usual neglected the work on the flower-beds that the season called for, they said little, secure in the thought that everything would be changed once Henry had come home. Indeed, now it was all settled, the sisters were filled with a sense of irresponsible elation such as they had not known for a long time; their tired heads were packed with projects of foreign travel and of all the surprises that usually attend it. Deborah would do a tour of German spas, and insisted upon going alone save only for her flag-pole. Tryphena was secretly and guiltily delighted. Now she could visit Spain, hear the southern nightingales out-sing the fountains, while the guitars struck by blind men filled the air with blinding light; perhaps she would go further afield, to Greece with her darling Adolphus's shade, even to India with her grandfather's.

Winter lasted an unconscionable long time that year; it was dark and cold for the February lambs, while in March the ground was still so hard frozen it half broke your back to turn the soil. Nor did any news come from America; but as Tryphena looked up at a foggy or raging sky she would say, it will come with the spring, and Henry himself will follow soon after. Meanwhile Deborah slipped back to her letter-writing.

On paper heavily black-edged for Lucius she wove once again a skein of intelligence westward as far as Ireland, east to Russia, and to the Celebes; in Neapolitan and Viennese drawing-rooms the prospect of the shameful Henry's return to Uptake was a lively topic of conversation as the days drew out.

One morning, as she woke, Tryphena heard the noise neither of wind nor of fog-horn; instead, sunlight, pale and cringing it is true, but still sunlight, was stealing between her curtains. It was the first spring morning ; to-day, she knew, there would come news from America.

Sure enough it did, in the shape of a rather bulky letter. In precise phrases Cousin Odo Chipchase reported from Washington the innumerable difficulties that the Legation had encountered in the tracing of Henry's whereabouts. He had been heard of in New Orleans, in a number of places along the Rio Grande, in Mexico, and lastly in California, where he had gone to prospect for gold. He had at length been tracked to San Francisco; there he had unfortunately met his end by drowning some six weeks since. The circumstances of his death were far from clear; he had fallen off the quay one foggy night in an ill-famed part of the port; earlier in the evening he had been seen in a gambling-house, where fortune had neglected him; the time of his end could be set with some precision, for the watch found on the body had stopped at twenty-five minutes past two. . . .

It could not, of course, be definitely described as a case of suicide, since there had been a number of brawls along the water-front that particular evening. It was known, nevertheless, that his prospecting venture had not been successful, and that at cards his luck had long ago left him. Nor, it seemed, had he received for the last two years any of the remittances which, under the agreement signed before he left England, had been regularly sent for him to a firm of lawyers in New York. Indeed, he had existed the last few weeks of his life upon the bounty of his slatternly landlady and of casual acquaintances contracted in disreputable circumstances. . . .

69

"I can't read any more," Deborah cried; "I can't see for tears."

Tryphena took the copious report in her shaking hand; after a moment's silence, broken only by Deborah's sniffs, "I can gather nothing more," she whispered, "save that Cousin Odo is thoroughly embarrassed in his official dignity by the necessity of enquiring into the miserable end of so disreputable a relative. He never approved of any among us, particularly as he could have no hope of coming into Uptake himself. He enquires with the prettiest show of solicitude imaginable what will become of the old place now that we are faced with the extinction of our line."

Deborah here broke into violent sobs. Tryphena went over and put an arm about the frail shoulders. A wave of the customary tenderness engulfed her; all her life her protective arm had encircled this delicate pretty sister; she herself, at once more lusty and less handsome, had never deserved, and certainly never obtained, any such comfort. . . .

Deborah clung to her with one hand; the other dabbed with a handkerchief at two streaming eyes.

"Whatever will become of Uptake now; what will become of me?"

The flow of Tryphena's tenderness lost half its volume. As usual, she thought with rising irritation, as usual Deborah is preoccupied with nobody's fate but her own.

"Little does it serve to cry"; her voice had grown harsh with exasperation; "this disaster is in a great part our fault, the fault of our pride and lack of mercy. We should never have hounded poor Henry out of his own, however vilely he might have behaved. God knows, I'm as guilty as you are in the matter."

Checking her tears, Deborah sprung round at her.

"That's indeed handsome of you, dear sister, when it was you who raged the fiercest of anyone against the poor angel. I always knew he wasn't the black sheep you made him out to be; and now you've killed him and ruined us all; you must be well pleased."

There was nothing to be gained by refuting these cruel charges; with time Deborah would recover her balance of mind, be ashamed for what she had said.

To curb her agitation, Tryphena went for a ride upon the hills toward the sea. Going out, she came upon Titmarsh, whom she hadn't seen for days. He looked as gay as a lark, was about to

70

impart the reason for his joy when he stopped short, seeing the distress in her face. Briefly she told him the news, then spurred away, unable to continue talking.

VIII

ON THE HILLS THE AIR WAS FILLED WITH THE promise of spring, the bleating of lambs, the cries of nesting plover, the scent of young clover. The throb of the sea was as remote and irregular as something heard in a dream; with the stillness of planets, the gulls would hang for minutes at a time in the bright air, then dive headlong for the distant waves.

She looked back, down into the valley where Uptake lay. She could just hear the whisper of the waterfall; the house blinked quiet in the sun, so lovely and serene a place, you would have said, no harm or trouble could ever come to it. Then as Tryphena gazed at the gleaming lawns and rich pastures the vision seemed to fade; there was no Uptake where she looked, no hothouses, temples, grottos, or cascades; only the salty marshes with their brackish pools and coarse reeds, the valley as it had been before wicked great-grandfather laid his talented hand upon it. All this beauty had been conjured by him out of the marshes, a fabulous achievement for his delight and that of his descendants. Now the fable was almost ended; Uptake no longer had any reason save its beauty, and even that had been created for the use and pleasures of great-grandfather's heirs alone.

On her return home Tryphena learnt from Hake that Deborah had come in hurriedly from a turn in the park and desired urgently to speak with her. Oho! Tryphena said to herself with a rising heart, the dear thing has come to her senses and is sorry for her cruel words.

Deborah, as usual, was seated at her davenport. She jumped up fiercely as Tryphena entered, spurned the outstretched hands. Tryphena stopped short, shocked by the white face lined with fury.

"What's happened? What's amiss?"

"You know very well, you wicked vengeful woman. Just because

71

I told you the plain truth about you this morning, you conceive a pretty plan to even accounts by frightening me so that I'll have heart failure and die. Well, you've probably achieved your wicked purpose. I've had a terrible attack, and only just contrived to drag my way back to the house. If it gives you any pleasure, I've been compelled to send urgently for the doctor; I only hope he arrives in time; my palpitations terrify me."

"Deborah, are you mad? What are you saying? I plan revenge against you for that silly squabble of this morning? I promise you that since I left you I have been out riding upon the hills."

"Don't act Miss Innocence to me. I go out to take a turn down by the lake; I come to the Philosopher's Hut, and idly walk inside, when suddenly the old Sage, who was long ago disconnected, as you well know, rises in the dark and strikes me with his stick, so that I fall insensible, and might have died there. And you pretend innocence when it was you who ordered the repair of his mechanism. Don't try to deny it. Albert heard you give the orders for the work to Titmarsh. And you can stand there so smug when you've contrived such a barbarity against a poor invalid." Deborah began to cry.

Tryphena tried fair words to calm her, but it was of no avail. Her temper began to give, her voice to rise with her sister's. Suddenly as they quarrelled a light of revelation came to her; she had devoted most of her life to the care of Deborah, accepting without question the general view that Deborah was dearer to her than any other soul upon earth. But now when all was vain, and the family doomed to extinction, why pretend to herself any longer? Deborah had always been hateful, selfish, interfering, jealous. Now she told her so.

Deborah stared at her for a moment in silence. "And you," she said slowly, "you are a monster. A monster, d'you hear; a sinner against God and against Nature. Not only do you strive to encompass your own sister's death, but you're an incestuous strumpet into the bargain. Well may you start; you thought I didn't know? Let me tell you, though it happened long years ago, I've never ceased thinking of it. You and your precious Adolphus. The dear angel, as innocent as the dawn, and you corrupting him with your harlotries."

"Say what you will; at least he infinitely preferred me to you;

72

"It was the first spring morning."

and that, dear sister, is in my belief the only reason why you can set yourself up in judgment against me."

Deborah rushed at her, but Tryphena held her off easily. Deborah suddenly collapsed in a fountain of hysterical tears; Tryphena left the room, dry-eyed but with a tormented heart. Strangely, it was not the lamentable scene that agonised her so much as the besmirching of her darling, and of those shameful moments of ecstasy so long gone. It was not until she was safely in her bedroom that she permitted herself the luxury of tears; once they had started, it was hard enough work to stop them.

That evening Deborah came to see her. "I've been reflecting," she said quite gently, "and reached a conclusion you'll no doubt share."

"You mean, Uptake is no longer big enough for the two of us?"

Deborah nodded. "And since I'm rather an invalid, and you've always thirsted for foreign travel——"

"It's your design that I should be the one to quit my home, isn't it? Well, dear sister, if one of us has to go, be assured it'll not be me. I would remind you I'm the eldest, for many years it's been my task to administer the estate——"

A squabble started afresh, till they were shrieking at each other like a couple of street harridans. At the height of the sordid tussle Tryphena with a wry smile said to herself, "Worthless Henry who never knew the meaning of genteel behaviour would have been astonished to learn that he was our last tie with proper deportment; now that he is dead there's no longer any reason for pretence."

Deborah at last quitted her, with everything left unresolved save their mutual hatred. Tryphena was then buffeted and shaken by such a storm of tears as she had not known since her youth; try as she would, nothing would stay it till the first light made even tears seem futile. Then, as she lay sleepless and swollen-eyed, the solution came to her attended by cock-crows.

When she communicated the idea to Deborah in the full light she expected to be dubbed mad; and indeed, she thought, after all I've gone through, there might be something in the charge. Deborah, however, took at once to the project. There was, she declared, nothing else that they could reasonably do in the circumstances. If they couldn't agree as to which one of them should have

74

"She came on Deborah, hunched upon a marble bench."

Uptake, who else could possess it? Certainly not that slimy parson from the Colonies.

It was a bright enough morning, but beyond noticing with some satisfaction a promise of wind in the mackerel sky, the sisters had no time to spare for the weather. There was much to be done in all too short a time—packing of clothes and of a few dear gee-gaws, the disposal of those pets that would not accompany them, the sending away of all the younger servants—to Tryphena's half-ashamed delight, several of them, including the lazy Tim, whom, the Lord knew, she'd scolded unmercifully in her time, left with noisy tears. As she stood alone in the colonnade she could hear their howls float back to her until they were well outside the park. . . .

Hake, it was arranged, should be set up in the little pub on the Bearminster road that he'd long coveted (and a nice muddle he was bound to make of it). Plummett and Drax would accompany their mistresses like attendant Furies—no escaping 'em. There remained only Titmarsh.

Tryphena summoned him as of old to the Museum, told him what was afoot, what was required of him; when he'd done their bidding, he'd have money enough to wander wherever his fancy commanded, to Cochin China where you could not see the tree-trunks for their armour of orchids, to Brazil where a lady was insulted by a present of orchids and rated a bunch of gillyflowers as the most devoted tribute. . . .

"Can't say as I likes it one little bit, my Lady, as the saying is; but if your Ladyship says so, orders is orders." He went off to make arrangements about the rarest of his precious blooms.

It was getting toward dusk when packing was finished and the two carriages had rolled up to the front door. The wind was rising, and the horses were stamping and whinnying as if they smelt the return of bad weather. The luggage was loaded on, some of it heavy and silent, some light and plaintive. At last everything was stowed, including Plummett and Drax, in their respective carriages; with that slightly unrecognisable air that all good servants put on before a journey, they sat dazed and disapproving of they knew not what; as yet they had no inkling of what was afoot.

Tryphena hurried back indoors to find Titmarsh and carry out her arrangements. In the piebald silence of the Etruscan hall she came on Deborah, hunched upon a marble bench; she was crying softly to herself. At the sight of her sister she jumped up, ran to her, seized her arm.

"We can't do it, we can't do it"; her voice tear-laden rose almost to a scream; "I'll agree to anything you wish. I'll live on one corner of the house, and we'll never cross each other's paths."

"You know it's no good." Tryphena shook off her arm. Deborah whimpered, then stared at her face.

"Sister, are you feeling well? Your eyes are glittering so strangely, your hands are hot and dry. I believe you have a fever. Hadn't you best repose a while?"

"Get to your carriage," Tryphena snapped harshly, "I've work to do." She never spoke to her sister again.

With everything necessary, Titmarsh was waiting miserably in the basement.

"Begging your Ladyship's pardon, we didn't ought; truly we didn't. It bain't right, not by a long chalk."

"When your views on ethics are required, Titmarsh, I shall be happy to call for them. Meanwhile there's much to be done before dark."

Titmarsh made as if to answer, but for once was daunted by the unholy light in her eye. They went about the work in hand. Somewhere, down a stilled passage, a door clattered in the strengthening wind.

They made a thorough job of it, finishing in the Blue Drawing-room. Tryphena took a last look at the fantastic mirrors; no more would she be able to escape into those fabulous pools that gleamed among the gilt rocks; no longer did she want to.

When all was done Titmarsh left her without a word. One second he was beside her, the next, she was alone in the deepening gloom. For a moment her inflexible spirit weakened; a wave of panic and regret submerged her. Then she pulled herself together and walked slowly out to her carriage.

It was blowing stiffly from the sea. A tatter of dark clouds raced across the early moon. Tryphena stepped into her carriage, whips were rattled in their holders, and the cortège moved off, down the drive over which sphinxes and caryatids stood sentinel, past the pools where doddering old carp still smacked their lips

77

"The carriages rolled out of the handsome gates."

at the thought of the rich morsels that had come to them in great-grandfather's day.

The carriages rolled out of the handsome gates, painfully climbed the ridge that commanded the park on the landward side. They stopped at the fork on the summit, where the Bearminster road parted company with that which led to Dropping Camden, through Lesser Riddance, and Caudle-on-the-Marsh. From the eminence where they waited they could look down upon Uptake, gleaming like a goddess among her groves, and inland toward Bearminster and the mines at Limber-le-Fosse. The setting sun cast its last beams upon the black regiments of hovels that under cover of smoke were advancing slowly across the verdant hills; every time Tryphena came up this road they seemed to have crept a little nearer; one day, she supposed, they would be slinking up the drive at Uptake, turning the statues into niggers; nobody wanted statues any longer, nor gardens either for that matter.

From Deborah's carriage, the parrot Hasdrubal squawked peevishly. The wind whipped the manes into the horses' eyes, making them toss their heads like dancers. Deborah was peering down toward the house, her fingers drumming on the window-glass. Tryphena, too, was in a fever, but one that worked otherwise upon her; if she so much as lifted a finger, she knew that she would scream till she went mad from her own noise.

Would it happen? Had something miscarried? She prayed that it hadn't, that it had. The lovely house, as lovely as a day-dream, a temple for youth and music, not for the cackles of two old spinsters: two old spinsters, without a home now, more ridiculous than ever they had been. No! Nothing moved down there, save the trees and cascades and the growing moonlight. She and Deborah must slink back absurdly into the mocking house, to die while it lived on.

She was just going to order the return, with anti-climax and elation in her heart, when she saw a glow in one of the fading windows. Suddenly a flame blossomed out of it like a lovely flower, was joined by another, and yet more, till there was a bed of great petunias. They swayed in the moaning wind, these flowery flames; next there came a low rumble, sparks like fireworks for a victory, and the whole of Uptake was roaring and crackling. Higher and higher rose the blaze; then suddenly above the tumult Tryphena

79

heard her sister laughing. It was the most terrifying sound of all, this peal of laughter, and she could suddenly stand the scene no longer. She ordered her coachman to drive on; Deborah's carriage took the other road. As they looked down for the last time toward the fiery valley, a drove of horses with tall plumes waving in the wind, and jockeys on their backs, seemed to be coursing madly round the blaze, in and out among the blood-red sphinxes.

The glare followed Tryphena miles down the road, shaming the cold moon, that now sailed high in the sky, and very far away.